MY FATHER IS A SERIAL KILLER

KILLER

A Psychological Thriller Novel
Written by Spencer Guerrero

Contents

TRIGGER WARNING

POTENTIAL SPOILERS BELOW

This book includes Murder, Death, Sexual Harassment, Sexual Assault, Domestic Abuse, Mental Abuse, Suicide, some graphic scenes of violence and some brief, non-graphic scenes of Child Abuse.

Reader Discretion Is Advised.

PROLOGUE

"I loved the idea that you saw me, fully intent on killing you and there was not a single thing you could do about it. You were helpless. You couldn't run, scream, or hide. It was too late. I was inches away from your terrified face and before you could even blink, you were finished forever. I only wish that I had done it much, much earlier and that you were somehow able to see how I butchered the people you loved most."

It was in the perfectly hellish small town of St. Devil. In the perfect suburban neighborhood that had freshly trimmed lawns, white picket fences and a clear, blue sky. The perfect peace was shattered by a vicious slaying that came swift and final. A grave murder that would cause near-eternal torment and devastation for an entire family.

It was pitch-black and raining. He stood outside in the muddy field with a trench coat while the torrential rain poured down on him like a waterfall. He firmly held the axe as he crept towards the house. He wore black gloves, a black face mask and shoe covers. He fully intended to get away with the vicious act he was about to commit. He would leave nothing behind. Not a single trace of dust, hair, fingerprints, or any other form of DNA. He was careful, meticulous, and precise when it came to the build-up of his sinister plan.

He carefully climbed over the backyard fence and used the axe to break in through the window. The relentless pitter-patter of the rain and the booming thunder masked the sharp crackle of the window breaking. She was in the living room and was walking back towards the kitchen when she saw him. She stood frozen and dropped her coffee mug on the floor, shattering it. Once he saw her face-to-face, all hell broke loose.

He lunged forward, swung high and ferociously cut into her shoulder before she could scream. She instantly collapsed to the ground and began hyperventilating. He retracted the blood-stained axe with a horrifying crunch and swung back down to her neck, squirting a fountain of blood all over her and himself. She choked on her own blood and died within minutes as he swung down two more times to slice her head off. He doubled over and breathed. The dark deed was done, and he was fully satisfied. He took out a black garbage bag from his coat pocket, and retrieved his trophy. Her shocked, decapitated head.

CHAPTER 1
PRESENT DAY

I needed to keep my promise. The promise I had made a long time ago. The promise that monsters never win. My mother was murdered, and I had reasons to believe that my Father was a serial killer. I know. It sounded insane. I didn't want to believe it. Who goes around thinking their own father is a serial killer? I was a true-crime enthusiast though, so I felt I had a pretty sharp instinct when it came to those things. *Serial-Killer-Related-Things.* Those instincts came in handy in a place called St. Devil. That's the name of my small town. The town where everything changed. The town you passed through on the way to a vacation destination. The town of two halves. One half was a perfect suburbia with clean-cut houses, neighborhoods, and playgrounds. The other half of town was comprised of half-empty shopping malls, long winding roads, unkept forests, endless farmland, abandoned houses, and corner strip clubs. We had drug dealers, junkies, doting wives, and white-collar husbands. We had it all.

The sun was setting as an orange streak of light was slowly fading across the horizon. I was parked in a mostly abandoned shopping plaza hiding in the back seat of my black sedan. I held my video camera horizontally as I recorded a unified SWAT team getting into defensive positions. Dozens of police officers formed a perimeter around a lone laundromat named *The Dirty Bin*. Customers were frantically running out as a long-haired, 40-year-old man with a scruffy gray beard ran towards the back of a dryer in the middle of the laundromat. He owned the place along with 2 other locations. It was alleged serial killer Kenneth Kilhouser, suspected of murdering 3 women across 3 years. His ex-wife, his sister-in-law, and his own daughter.

That's what I did. For the last several years, I followed grisly murder cases that involved degenerate nutjobs like Kenneth Kilhouser. I worked as a freelance journalist specializing in true crime and did a fair bit of the social media influencer thing on the side. The time I spent on making 3-minute videos and soundbites usually rewarded me with a free water bottle or a package of gluten-free fig bars.

Hey everyone! Today we're gonna be talking about the case of the ex-convict husband who sliced his wife and his dog in half with a buzzsaw...but first a word from my sponsor: Yummy Tummy Bars!

It was terrible. I knew it was, but it was the only way I could justify making those videos. The truth was...nobody read anymore. This was especially true in St. Devil. Nobody picked up a newspaper and nobody wanted to pay $10 a year to get past the paywall to read online. The only way I could truly inform the masses was through various forms of social media. At times I hated myself for having to make gimmicky videos, but there was a reason I did all this. It was to get assholes like Kenneth Kilhouser who belonged 6 feet underground. I was the one who received an anonymous tip that he was seen burying Diane Kilhouser's detached head in Meadow Lakes Park. I tipped off the police and they found security camera footage of him dragging her dead body along with her head. He was seen moving through the outskirts of the country club near Meadow Lakes in the dead of night.

I held my camera steady as my heart swelled in anticipation. I was about to see him get lit up like a Christmas tree.

It was an adrenaline-pumping thrill seeing a police shoot-out. It was the only time I felt everything hang in the balance. Where a stray bullet could penetrate my skull and end it all just like that. My husband hated that I attended these things. It was incredibly dangerous and terrifying of course, but necessary. I needed to see what would happen to Kenneth up close and personal. I had been writing about a potential serial killer in St. Devil for months after the *Triple K Murders*. I even spoke with Kenneth once at the same laundromat. I questioned him regarding the murders of his family. He had been strange and very cold. He spoke in a gravelly tone and had a wet, throaty cough that made me want to gag. He had all the makings of a serial killer. A lone outcast who didn't understand how to be social or normal. It made my job that much harder later on when it came to my own Father. He was anything but an outcast.

Kenneth Kilhouser come out with your hands up! We have you surrounded!

Do not try anything or we will shoot!

Come out slowly! Final warning!

The fully armed authorities were ready to blow that guy to bloody bits if he didn't comply. I knew that they wanted nothing more. He was a dark menace and he needed to be ended. I didn't believe in rehabilitating serial killers, rapists, or other murderers. If their mind was twisted enough to commit the darkest deeds of humanity in the first place, they didn't deserve to live. I had seen enough cases and crimes. These people never changed. Why would they? Deep down, they wanted to be right. They wanted to be right about butchering innocent souls.

My heart began beating faster and faster with anticipation as Kenneth remained inside the laundromat. A second later, there was a quick motion inside. Kenneth had moved to another spot with cover.

Final warning!

Nothing. Kenneth did not intend to live. As soon as I heard bullets ripping through the glass of the laundromat I ducked but held my video camera up to catch the explosive scene. I heard the thundering crackle of rifle shots being discharged in every direction as I closely shut my eyes and waited for it to be over.

I'm hit!

An officer shouted out in pain. I couldn't believe it. Kenneth was armed and he had managed to shoot a cop. I heard the crunch of footsteps inching forward on the gravel of the parking lot as the bullet fire intensified. Minutes later, it stopped. I peeked my head up and saw an absolute storm of shells littered across the line of police officers and SWAT team members. Bullet holes had shredded through nearly every inch of the laundromat. Washing machines, dryers and vending machines were annihilated in the aftermath. Kenneth's body was a disgusting mess of blood and brain matter as he laid down lifeless across the darkened linoleum floor. I made sure to save the video and quietly laid down in my car as my heart wouldn't stop racing.

Kenneth Kilhouser is dead. The horror is over. The serial killer behind the Triple K Murders has been brought to justice. Monsters never win.

I tweeted. I had over 2000 notifications in minutes as I muted my phone. One message snuck by.

You're insane, Venus Duarte. Only you would want to see Kenneth being executed.

I was sure that I was. The horror that Kenneth Kilhouser inflicted on others was over, but not the horrors that were inflicted on me.

Monsters never win. Yeah. Right. I thought. I didn't even believe it myself.

I was fortunate to live in a peaceful suburban neighborhood with a perfectly modest one-story house. We had the two semi-old, dependable cars in the driveway, the kind next-door neighbors who baked apple pie and the young elementary school kids who rode bikes while simultaneously trying to catch digital monsters on their tablets. So much innocence. If only I had been worried about things like that when I was a kid. I wished that my only concern was that I wasn't able to catch the imaginary monster out in the wild. Unfortunately I had to deal with a real monster.

I was a stocky, dark-haired brunette with dark brown eyes and tan skin. By all means I was a Latina archetype because of my mother Violet, who was Venezuelan. But I wasn't feisty. I didn't like to be called that. I just wasn't afraid of getting things done, even if I actually was deep down. My trick was to trick myself into thinking I had courage. That usually worked for me. My husband Arthur was also Hispanic, but his family was born in Northern Nicaragua. They had a lighter complexion. As a result he had light brown hair and sparkly green eyes. He was four inches taller than me, and he didn't like me mentioning his *dad bod*. He had a beer gut and a receding hairline, but I didn't care. He was my Arthur. He was solid, steady, and dependable. He was what I needed until he decided to make things complicated for me.

The inside of my house was simple. The living room had an open-concept space that integrated the living room, dining area, and kitchen. The only furniture I had was a low-profile, charcoal-gray sofa with clean lines, a coffee table crafted from a single slab of brown stone, and a small dining table surrounded by a set of sculptural chairs. I had large windows which allowed natural sunlight to pour in, illuminating the whole house. Which made me feel better when I had my bouts of panic and anxiousness. I didn't like the dark. In my experience, bad people always did bad shit in the dark. It was always dark in the *Box*.

Arthur was at his desk, clicking and typing away on his fancy work laptop. He was a software developer for a major grocery chain, and he worked from home. Which meant I couldn't escape his questioning when I went out on my little danger quests. He saw me sneak in, sweaty and gross. He lifted his head and folded his arms. I mocked him and did the same.

"Hey," Arthur said.

"Hey."

"Where were you?"

"I went to the market." I slid over to him and sat on his lap.

"What you'd get?"

I stared at him for several seconds. My mind was drawing nothing but blanks.

Shit, shit, shit, shit.

"You know, almond milk. Stuff that married people buy," I responded.

"You went to another crime scene."

"I did not. Why would you assume that?"

"You're very sweaty, and you smell like something's burning."

"I'm not burning. Obviously."

"I already know that that is the smell of bullets. It must've been a lot of guns." I saw the concern etched on his face. I couldn't lie to him about that. He already knew anyway.

"Okay, fine. I went."

"Why, Venus? Why do you do this?" Arthur sighed.

"We've already talked about this. It's my job. I'm an adult and I can do what I want. I know that you're my husband, but I am your wife. I am not your prisoner."

"Of course you're not Venus, but I can take care of you. You don't have to do that anymore. You don't have to put yourself in danger."

"If I didn't have this, I'd go nuts. What would I do all day?"

"You can relax and cook. You can do other hobbies. You can do whatever you want," Arthur chimed.

"I'm not gonna relax and cook for 12 hours a day. I'll stick a bullet in my head." I slid off of him and walked to the kitchen.

"What about chess? Do you like playing chess?"

"I don't know how to play chess."

"What's that board game you loved to play with Vera then?"

"Honey, that's *Parcheesi.*"

"Shit, that's right! Why don't you play that? It looks fun. I can play with you on my breaks."

I love you Arthur, but I don't think being holed up in the same house every single day for 24 hours a day would be good for our marital health.

"I don't really wanna play that. I'm sorry."

"I'm trying here. I just want you to be safe."

"I am safe. I've been doing this for a very long time." I took out a bottle of wine and poured myself a glass. I was gonna need it.

"Who was it this time? Can you at least tell me that?"

"It was Kenneth Kilhouser. The alleged serial killer. Well, not so alleged anymore."

"Oh Jesus, that psycho? Isn't he the one who chopped off their heads and kept them as trophies? Arthur stood up and followed me.

"Yeah that's him, but he buried their heads. He didn't keep them long. I'm guessing."

Sometimes serial killers were so mentally twisted that they sexually violated the severed heads of their victims. Kilhouser might've done that, but I hoped not. It was his family. Then again, the odds of him being a sick enough bastard to do something like that were in his favor.

"So, what happened? What did the police do?"

"There was a uh...police shoot-out. Before you freak out, I'm fine. It was quick and intense, but yeah it was under control. I wasn't near it, but I got some great footage."

"A police shoot-out?! I knew it. You stress me out when you tell me this shit. You could have been killed."

"Yeah, but I wasn't. Okay?" I took a sip of my wine and winked at him.

"Don't try to be funny right now. What footage did you get? Are you going to show people that he got shot and killed?" Arthur had disgust in his voice, and I softly shoved him. He was beginning to seriously annoy me.

"No, Arthur. I'm not showing that. Only the build-up. My god. Is the interrogation over?" I practically threw my empty glass in the sink and started to stomp away before he put his hand on my shoulder.

"Look, I'm sorry for caring so much but I do. You're my wife and I want you to be alive for the next 40 years. Is that too much to ask?"

Arthur had a slight mist in his eyes. I didn't like seeing him like that. I wrapped my arms around his waist and rubbed his back so he would feel better.

"I will be alive for the next 40 years and you will too, okay? Kenneth is dead and it's all over for now," I said softly.

"Okay. I love you, Venus. Even if your stubbornness is never-ending."

"I love you too and yes it is never-ending."

In hindsight I should've been more grateful for my marriage to Arthur. There were others who weren't so lucky.

I always had trouble sleeping from an early age. I don't remember when it started but I knew it had gone on for a long time. I had problems shutting off my mind and my ever-revolving thoughts.

Why do I always feel like something bad is supposed to happen to me?

Does Arthur secretly hate me?

Is there something wrong with me?

Add to that a burning sensation in my chest that ebbed and flowed at night, and I was sure that I had insomnia. Sometimes the only way to cure it was to wake Arthur. I knew he wanted to strangle me for waking him up at 3 AM but he never said it. He'd never say it. On that particular night, I had a dream about Vera. I always seemed to dream about her. She appeared like a ghost and spoke to me about things

I never remembered. I used to hate dreaming about her but after it happened, I almost looked forward to it. Regretfully, I didn't see her much after my marriage to Arthur. Whenever I saw her I got the same feeling I had when we were kids. I loved my little sister but her very existence reminded me of the horrible torment we went through for so long. Whenever I saw her face...I saw his.

I rolled over from my side of the bed and stared at his hairy back. I softly caressed his little hairs until he woke up with a loud groan.

"Were you sleeping?" It was a dumb question.

"Yeah," he answered groggily.

"Are we alright?"

"What do you mean?" Arthur turned over with his eyes closed.

"Nothing. It's okay."

"Don't do that. Just tell me."

I readjusted my pillow and tucked my hair behind my ears.

"I know you hate it when I go on my danger quests as you call them. So, I was wondering if you were still mad about that."

"I'm not."

"Okay."

Arthur turned back over.

"Are you going back to sleep?"

"Yeah."

"Sorry."

"It's okay."

"We can talk more in the morning I guess."

"I'm...I'm hungry." Arthur's stomach growled.

I giggled.

"I feel like I can eat a baby elephant."

"Do you want something now?"

"No it's okay. We can go out tomorrow."

"Good because you're crazy if you think I'm going to leave this bed at this hour." I grinned.

Arthur scoffed.

"Hey," he said in a serious tone.

"Yeah?"

"I really want to have a baby." Arthur turned and shuffled up. He squinted his eyes at me.

"I know."

"Have you thought about it?"

"I don't know if I'm ready for that yet, Arthur," I said defensively.

I didn't like it when he brought it up. I didn't think I was in a good mental state to be a mother. Hell, I was still grieving the death of my own mother who was savagely murdered. Hot flashes and panic attacks regularly came in the night after her murder. I usually woke up in a cold sweat, hyperventilating and mumbling incoherent words which always freaked out Arthur. All he could do was hold me until it stopped. It became less frequent after a while but only because I hid it from him. Sometimes I woke up earlier than him and would tip-toe to the bathroom. I'd sit on the bathroom floor and close my eyes until it was over. I usually cried to myself. I didn't want Arthur to see me like that all the time. It must've been exhausting for him.

He was my rock, but I didn't want to break him. I needed him whole because I knew for a fact that I wasn't.

"I get it," Arthur mumbled.

I knew he was upset. It's not that I didn't want a baby. I wanted a child with Arthur, but I was afraid. I was deeply afraid of raising my child in a dark, brutal world. The world I knew. The world I regularly lived in. A lot of the gory crimes I talked about and reported on involved children. I would feel nothing but terror if I brought a child into the world.

"I'm sorry, Arthur," I offered.

"It's fine, I guess."

If only you knew.

A few hours later, I woke up and saw that Arthur was still asleep. I decided to go back to bed because I knew what awaited me later on in the day. We had many talks about having a baby throughout the years and I was all for it until my mother was butchered. All of a sudden, I didn't feel like having one anymore. My mind was in a serious panic and all the fears and anxieties I had in the early years of my life came storming back. It was like I had gone back in time. Arthur was just getting up when I fell back asleep. I dreamt of my mother that time, not Vera. It was the rainy night of her demise. A man had broken into her house and had sliced her up with an axe. She was dead within seconds. The police believe the murderer did it that night because the heavy rain and thunder would cover up any noises he made.

I believed that theory. The body was discovered by her neighbor Sandra the next morning when she noticed that she hadn't gone out to get her packages near the front door. She had gone around the back and that's when she noticed the sliding door to the backyard had been shattered. Everyone in the community heard Sandra's horrified shrieking when she spotted my mother's headless body and the splattering of red splotches everywhere. It was a gruesome bloodbath.

I still remember when I found out. I still remember my chest exploding with pain and my wailing when I realized that the headless murder victim in front of me was my own mother. I was in a grief-ridden daze that entire day and the following week. I couldn't believe it. She was not only dead but murdered. Once I stopped asking myself *why*? I started asking myself *who*?

When I got up for the second time, I found Arthur playing computer games at his desk. He had been playing for several months now for hours on end during the weekends. I knew when he was playing because he was wearing his fancy headset with enlarged earmuffs and was yelling profanities at the screen. I could never tell if he was yelling at actual people or at the fictional characters in the game. When he saw me walk in he slid one earmuff out of his ear.

"Sorry for waking you. How'd you sleep?" I asked innocently.

"Fine."

"Are we still going out?"

"Yeah, I'm still hungry. Have you thought more about the baby?"

I blinked rapidly. I wasn't expecting that question again so soon. I figured he would've waited until breakfast at least. I thought carefully to formulate a good answer. I sat down on the sofa and crossed my legs.

"I need more time. I still feel like my mother was murdered yesterday. She would've been the grandma to our child. She was robbed of that. I still can't believe she's gone." I choked up, but quickly regained my composure.

"I know, Venus. You might not believe me, but I miss her too. Even if she was a bit difficult at times. I loved your mother." Arthur took off his headset and shut off his computer.

"You're a saint for dealing with all that." I grinned.

"I did it for you."

"I know."

"I'm getting old, Venus. I feel like my clock for having a baby is dwindling. I don't wanna be 60 when my kid is 12. You're 33 and I'm 38. Truth is, I'm tired of gaming all day. This can't be it for us. I feel like there's an entire aspect of our lives that we're missing. Don't you feel that? Am I crazy? Please tell me if I am," Arthur pleaded.

I wanted kids, but I didn't want to bring them into a family that was cursed. I couldn't tell Arthur that. I couldn't tell him the truth.

"You're not crazy, Arthur. You know I want to be a mother. You know I want to have a family with you. We talked about it when we were younger."

"Then I need to know if we're gonna have a baby or not. I'm not trying to sound harsh, but I need to know, Venus. No matter what, I love you. I swear that I still love you, Venus." Arthur came over and sat down next to me. He took my hands and squeezed them tight. I didn't believe him. I didn't believe that Arthur would still love me or look at me the same if we didn't have a child. I knew that as we grew older with no children, he would resent me. There was no way he wouldn't. Our home would feel so empty, and he'd blame me for it. Looking back, I could've been wrong, but I didn't believe that back then. I believed that Arthur would hate me if I didn't have our baby. I wished he would've forgotten about the whole thing, but he never did. I couldn't have him hating me. I didn't need any more pain and heartbreak in my life. I needed peace. I needed stability. I needed love. I needed him.

"Let's have a baby then."

Arthur smiled and pulled me in. He hugged me so tight I felt the sheer warmth of his love spreading all over me. I hadn't felt that way in a long time. I didn't know what else to say to him. I wanted him to be happy, even if I wasn't at the moment. I said what I had to, to appease him for the time being. Even if my own mother was devastatingly cruel to me at times, I wanted to become one. I wanted to do better. But things grew far more complicated. There were far more important things at stake than starting a family amidst the chaos and the ruins of the tragedy that followed.

CHAPTER 2
1 YEAR EARLIER

I had an uncle once named David Snow. He was a short, skinny man who was bald. He had beady eyes and wore black, circular glasses. He was mild-mannered and lived a simple life. He rarely caused a ruckus, never instigated any drama, and never gossiped. He had a close relationship with my Father and seemed to be doing just as well as the rest of us.

It turned out we were all dead wrong in the most horrific way possible. One day, out of the blue, he was found with a rope tied around his neck. Uncle David killed himself and no one really understood why. Father was beyond devastated. He was never the same after his little brother's death. He changed and became worse. He became a monster. My mother said he became who he truly was after David's death. Whatever the case was, I was determined to find the truth behind it all.

My family tended to reunite on many shitty occasions. I guess that was every family though. That time it was the funeral of Barry's wife, Caroline. Barry was my brother-in-law, Arthur's sibling. It was at a small church which was situated in a large open field.

My family and I sat in a solid oak pew inside where it was dark. There was stained glass which casted colorful vibrant patterns of light inside. Candles flickered nearby as a group of ministers surrounded a sacred statue. I stared up at the high ceiling and thought about how solemn the whole thing was. The atmosphere was heavy with sorrow and the air was thick with grief. Arthur was with Barry. He was sobbing and on his knees as he prayed at the altar.

I sat next to Vanya Reyes, my aunt. She was in her 40s and loved to drink. She had light brown hair with blonde highlights that reached down to the mid-section on her back. She had puffy brown eyes and even puffier lips. She was on the heavier side and liked to wear long, floral dresses to accentuate her curves. She was someone who needed to be the best dressed at every function. Which meant that she was typically overdressed but good luck telling her that. She also wore a dozen glittery rings and bracelets on her hands and arms to attract male suitors. All Aunt Vanya wanted was to be rich, to drink and to look *fantabulous*. She had no problem admitting that to anyone who would listen. I loved her even more for it.

My little sister Vera was humbler. She was a sweet-natured girl who focused on her studies. She was slender with glossy pink hair and soulful, honey-colored eyes. We had an age gap that was more than 10 years. I usually saw Vera as a daughter rather than a sister. I loved her from the moment she was born and always tried my best to shield her from the cruelties of the world. A part of me died forever when I failed.

Violet Snow, my mother, was still alive during Caroline's funeral. She was as critical as ever too. She was a scantily clad woman who always wore sunglasses, even indoors. She dressed the exact opposite of my aunt. She typically wore black and plain clothing with no markings. She said she didn't like attracting too much attention to herself. That was especially true on that day.

"This is too depressing. I need a drink. Where are the drinks?" Vanya begged.

"They don't serve drinks at funerals," I answered.

"Are you serious? That's the one freaking thing they should serve," Vanya grumbled.

"You didn't lose anyone. You need to relax," my mother snapped.

"Get me a drink and I will," Vanya replied.

"Stop behaving like a child," my mother scolded.

Vanya folded her arms and sulked. I looked at Vera who appeared anxious and winked.

"Are you okay?"

"Yeah, I'm good," Vera whispered.

"The girl is fine, leave her be."

"Relax, mom. It was one question."

The front doors swung open blinding everyone with sunlight.

"Who the hell is coming at this time? They have no consideration for anyone at all. Christ," my mother whined.

"Oh shit, it's him." Vanya gasped.

We all stared ahead and saw him. The patriarch. Dennis Snow. My Father. It had been many years since we had last seen him. It was a shock to us all when he arrived. He was a towering blonde man with bloodshot emerald eyes and a fit, rectangular body cultivated from his college football days. He was the type of guy who took up all the space in a hallway because of his massive block-like body. He had a way of sucking the air out of the room. I nervously tapped my foot and tried to suppress the butterflies in my stomach as he sauntered over to us.

"Hell of a place to have a family reunion, huh? Violet, Vanya, Venus, and Vera. The gang is all here. The *V Girls*." Father smirked.

"I'm surprised you made it. It's been years. Why the hell did you come back?" My mother hissed.

"Not happy to see me?" Father swung out his arms to indicate his apparent affection towards us.

"Why the fuck would I be happy to see you?" My mother asked.

My mother was not one to mince words, especially at her age. Vera nudged closer to me and held my hands. It was ice cold in the church, but I was sure she held onto me for another reason. One that involved a crippling fear of the man who stood in front of us.

"Hey Dennis. It's good to see you. You're still working out?" Vanya eyed his veiny biceps up and down. I wanted to hurl. She was always a little too warm towards my Father after everything that happened. It was off-putting.

"Always, Vanya. I need to outlive the gremlin that is my ex-wife." Father laughed.

"Hush! We are in a place of worship and there is a funeral taking place. You idiot." My mother was about to implode. Father waved her off.

"No one's paying attention to me, Violet. You can relax. Before I forget, I want to talk to you about selling some old properties in your name. Maybe you can make me your special lemonade."

So that's why he came back.

"I'm not making you any lemonade. We can discuss all of that later. We are at a *funeral*." She practically shouted.

"You see? Now people are paying attention because of your scandalous behavior. I'm going to make the rounds before people remember I was married to you." Father slid away, but before he did he pointed at me and winked.

"Good seeing you, Venus. You and your sister look as lovely as ever."

"Fuck off dad," I mumbled.

"Please don't be mean. I don't want him to get mad," Vera whispered.

"If I wanted to get him mad I would've shouted it." I squeezed Vera's hand.

She was too innocent for her own good. I was glad that she had me around. I wouldn't let the world or him swallow her up. My Father went to speak with Walter Campbell, his old neighbor. A warm, wealthy man who wore top-of-the-line suits and drove the coolest cars imaginable. Walter's most prized possession was a 1972 Firebird. My Father loved him because he felt he was on the same level as him. Walter was shorter and thinner than my Father, but he had shining, soft brown hair, dark yet kind eyes and a winning smile. Walter was friends with everyone like my Father.

I didn't figure out what was wrong with Walter until later. Everyone had something. A dark impulse, a scandalous secret, a bad childhood or maybe a weird foot fetish. Everyone had *something* wrong with them. The easiest thing I ever did was assume that everyone was fucked up in *some* way.

"Why were you being nice to him, Vanya? Have you lost your mind?" My mother asked.

"Oh relax, I was just keeping things civil. *Funeral*, remember? I still hate him for the complete asshole that he is," Vanya firmly stated.

"Whatever. I need fresh air after that bullshit." My mother stood up and rushed outside. Fresh air meant that she was going to smoke several cigarettes. A habit that came up after her divorce. My Father always had a way of riling up my mother. Sometimes all it took was a reminder that he still existed. That's why Vera didn't live with our mother anymore. I didn't trust her to look after my little sister. After several arguments that involved shouting and cussing, my mother finally gave in and agreed. She never admitted to having depressive episodes and never would, but Vera saw the pills. She told me everything. I would've taken Vera in myself, but Vanya begged me to house her. She was shockingly more stable, but she tended to drink until she saw stars. Vera promised to keep an eye on her and occasionally trashed the alcohol she bought. Aunt Vanya never had a clue. None of us even realized how much of a drunk she was because of how functional she could be. She only cut down drastically because her niece lived with her.

I never understood why funeral services ran so long. There was nothing to do. I could only be sad for so long before it got boring. It sounded insensitive but I had been at the church for 5 hours. My sadness meter had run out. I ended up watching Vera lifelessly play *Parcheesi* on her phone. I was so engrossed that I hadn't realized that Vanya had left my side. I glanced up and spotted her talking to Barry. He was an athletic, heavily tattooed police officer with a shaved head. When I first met him I thought he was a Neo-Nazi. When he told me he was a cop I thought he had no business enforcing the law. If Arthur was the good apple, one could guess who Barry was.

Arthur was not around so I kept an eye on them. They seemed to be having a normal conversation at first until I heard Barry speaking louder and louder.

I'm sorry. I'm really sorry. Please Vanya. I'm trying here. Barry pleaded.

Vanya did not look comfortable. When she tried to step away from him, he held out his hand and gripped her elbow which made her jump. No one was really paying attention except for me and my mother who was dashing across the church to get to them.

Oh dear.

Before I sprang up, my mother was already telling Barry to quietly *fuck off*. Barry was clearly not *fucking off*, so my mother shoved him while Vanya tried to keep the peace. Before I could get there Barry stormed off and went outside. I rubbed Vanya's shoulder to comfort her.

"Hey, what happened? Are you okay?"

"No she's not okay. That violent animal put his hands on her again. He has no control. You shouldn't have married Arthur. I told you. I told you from the very beginning." My mother paced.

"I didn't marry Barry, mom. Jesus Christ. He just lost his wife. Can we please keep calm?" I urged. I felt my stomach rapidly expanding and I wanted everything to remain peaceful before I had a panic attack in the middle of Caroline's funeral.

"It's okay, I'm fine. Barry has issues. I understand that. I'm just a little surprised this happened again." Vanya shuddered.

I hugged her tightly while my mother rolled her eyes.

"You've heard the rumors haven't you?" My mother asked.

"Not this shit again," I begged.

"Caroline was shot to smithereens with a shotgun. Who owns a shotgun? Barry does. She was also pregnant. Married men love shooting their pregnant wives. It's a notable statistic."

Who owns a shotgun? A fair amount of people.

"Barry might be very mentally ill, but I think you are too."

"That's exactly what I want to hear from my own daughter." My mother turned away and grimaced.

"I didn't mean it mom. Whatever, I'm going to fix this." I sighed.

I tried not to hold grudges, but it was hard to forgive what my mother had done to me. It was hard having to endure the raging abuse of both parents. I could never seek refuge with either one. I only took refuge with Vera.

I went outside and saw a small crowd of churchgoers reciting Bible verses. I worked my way around them and spotted Arthur speaking with Barry near a large tree in hushed tones. I charged ahead and was fully prepared to back up my husband.

"Are you drunk? You know how you are when you're drunk. You tend to ramble and do stupid shit."

"No, I'm not drunk. I'm not gonna drink at my dead wife's funeral. I'll have plenty of time to do that later."

"You can't be treating people like that, Barry. You're a police officer, man. You know better than this." Arthur reprimanded.

"Just because I'm a cop, don't mean shit. I got friends that treat people bad all the time. It don't mean jack shit. None of this shit means shit." Barry argued.

Well said as always, Barry.

"Your friends are bad. You aren't."

"At least you don't have to be. You can try to be better than them," I chimed in.

"You don't wanna be hearing this, little lady. I'm sorry about your Aunt Vanya. I shouldn't have said anything. I don't know how to talk to people. I was never taught."

A grown man who was a cop who didn't know how to talk to people. I was terrified of Barry and the dangers he could potentially unleash. He had *very* deadly weapons at his disposal and an unstable mind. He was a ticking time bomb. A perfect recipe for an absolute disaster.

"Forget about talking then. Venus' family came here to support you during your time of grieving. Look, what happened to Caroline was devastating. I'm in a lot of pain too. I loved her like she was my sister. Whoever murdered her robbed you of your future with her. I'm so sorry, brother. I will get you the help you need and I'm always here for you. You can't lash out at other people. You need to leave Vanya alone. Whatever happened in the past can stay there. It's done. Forget about it."

Barry broke down and thrusted his head into Arthur's chest as he wrapped his arms around him. He started bawling. The churchgoers noticed and looked at him with sympathetic eyes.

"Fuck man. I lost Caroline. *My* Caroline. I lost my baby. Who kills a pregnant woman?! Who?! It's not fucking fair!" Barry sobbed.

"I know. I know it isn't."

I didn't envy Arthur one bit. What the hell were you supposed to say to your own brother in that situation? His pregnant wife was shot and brutally murdered in one of the most tragic crimes ever committed in St. Devil's history. One thing was very clear. Barry's normal life and his will to live ended the day Caroline died. I didn't blame him. When the future is ripped from you in the worst way possible, what else is left? Nothing but pain, grief and a never-ending darkness strangling your heart.

The rain came fast and heavy. We all ran inside and dried ourselves off with leftover napkins from the catering service. Vanya took one glance at Barry and quickly turned heel. My mother scowled at him as he drowned himself in his own misery while he sat next to his brother. Father stared at him and softly shook his head, disapprovingly. Either he knew something I didn't, or my Father was a real top-tier asshole. Barry definitely had his issues, but my Father needed to look in the mirror for once.

Things felt very odd the day after the funeral. The sadness obviously lingered but it was strangely silent, like there was something terrible that had happened that I didn't know about yet. I stared at the clock in my living room and waited. My gut was bursting with anticipation. It felt like a deadly worm was slowly gnawing away at my insides. I breathed in and out before I had a full-blown panic attack for the thousandth time. The torrential downpour and my husband's calmness did nothing to make me feel better. I wanted to leap out at him and shake him. There was something wrong and we needed to find out what it was. I couldn't do that of course. He'd admit me into a mental hospital. I couldn't go there. I could never go there. It reminded me of the *Box*. I needed to keep my panicked thoughts to myself, as I often did.

I always felt like my body knew the bad things that were gonna happen in my life before they happened. I didn't know how or why, but it knew and tried to warn me. Unfortunately, there was absolutely nothing I could do to stop the events that changed my life forever. Arthur was click-clacking away at his computer when we heard a booming knock at the door. I already knew who it was. He tended to sound like he was trying to destroy front doors when he knocked.

I swung the door open and found Father standing there. He looked shell-shocked and wasn't smiling. A rarity. His eyes were puffy, and his lips trembled.

"Hey sweetheart." Father cleared his throat.

This is it. This is the worm gnawing at my insides.

"Hi dad. What's wrong?"

"Venus...Violet is dead. Your mother is dead."

"What? What are you talking about?"

"A police detective informed me. She was murdered, Venus."

Time stood still as I collapsed to the floor. My head was spinning and everything around me felt like it was crumbling. I saw Arthur rushing to me from the corner of my eye. He shoved my Father, and they exchanged harsh words. All I heard was a deafening ringing in my ears so I couldn't make out what was said. All I knew was that Arthur thought my Father had done something to me. When he realized what the news was, he bent down and held me as tightly as he could. Tears poured out of my eyes like a waterfall and my chest felt like it was being crushed by a 200 pound dumbbell.

I already knew it was true. My body was attempting to forewarn me. Arthur picked me up and took me to the sofa. Father entered and closed the door. He sat down alongside me and tried to hug me, but I immediately pushed him away. I shrieked an incoherent flurry of angry words directed at him. He deflected it and took it with a slight grin. A shit-eating grin. I wanted to punch him so hard. I wanted to smash his face until my knuckles were bloodred. I wanted to break his jaw so he could never smile again, but he was like Teflon. I scurried outside to my backyard and told both men not to follow me. I needed time alone. I sat on my tire swing and didn't care that it was still showering. I stared at the evil, dark grey sky and sobbed. My mother was gone. I didn't know how she was killed but I knew it was bad. I knew she died in a very bad, evil way.

A barrage of bad memories flooded my mind. All the times my Father had abused and hit me. All the times Violet had mentally abused me and criticized me. She criticized my clothing and my fast-food eating habits. She hated my decision to marry Arthur and my decision to take Vera away from her. She made me feel bad about not having children and told me being a mother was the most important thing I would ever do. She told me to give up the true crime reporting and told me it was a horrific job. My mother didn't make things easy for me a lot of the time. I caught myself and wondered why I felt so grief-stricken that my mother had died. I soon realized why.

I was only 10 years old when it happened. My Father had an important phone call relating to his real estate business while I was trying to get his attention. I was playing around with a plastic doll and waving it in his face. He kept shooing me away, but I was persistent. I was born a stubborn child. My mother used to say that I wouldn't stop crying as a baby until one of them picked me up and acknowledged the fact that I existed. Things didn't change much as I entered adulthood.

I was swinging that doll around like a helicopter by its hair and that's when it all went wrong. My heart plunged when the doll slipped out of my fingers and hit my Father's nose. Somehow, his nose started bleeding and he was forced to end the call after he grunted in pain. He squeezed his nostrils tightly together with one hand while he glared at me with darkened eyes. He menacingly stood up and towered over me, casting a very scary shadow. I froze in absolute fear and my legs turned into concrete. He lunged towards me with his other hand and grabbed my neck. His fingers pressed into my fragile skin, and I found myself gasping for breath as my eyes watered, blurring my vision. All I could think was *why*? Why was my own Father hurting me? It was an accident. I didn't want to see my Father bleed. I just wanted his attention for once.

I tried to squeak out that I was sorry, but his rage was unwavering. I really thought I was going to die. I began to think about the life I had lived and as a 10-year-old child I told myself that perhaps it was for the best. If I was dead I would no longer experience the pain of living with a monster. I would no longer have to endure my Father's fits of wrath. I would no longer have to sleep with terror in my heart, worried what the next day would bring.

My mother's screams broke my line of thought. She rushed forward, arms stretched out and sunk her nails deep into my Father's hands. He yelled out and dropped me. I fell to the floor, my ears buzzing. I clutched my throat and tried to swallow every breath I could gather. My mother had saved me. She tore him off but made herself a target.

"What the fuck are you doing to my daughter?!"

"That dumb little bitch made me bleed!"

"She's a little girl! You will never touch her again!" My mother commanded.

"Come here, Violet." Father threatened.

She looked at me with fearful eyes and I began to crawl towards her. She quickly waved me away.

"Go to your room Venus and lock the door!"

"But mom," I croaked.

"Now!"

I did as she said and never looked back. I sprinted to my room, locked the door, and hid under the bed. I heard a volcanic argument ensue between my parents as I tried to shut them out by putting my hands over my ears. I felt vibrations through the floor. Someone had fallen to the ground or was pushed. By the time it was over I had heard several pieces of glass breaking, walls being punched, and someone being slammed against a door. It was one of the most horrifying experiences of my life. It wasn't the first time either. I didn't live with a man. I lived with an extremely violent force of nature.

Despite everything, I did love my mother. The throbbing pain in my chest that vibrated throughout my entire body refused to go away. That was proof enough that whatever love I had for her was prevailing. My Father was to blame. He abused her and scared her into being someone she wasn't. A critical, bitter woman. Arthur came out and wrapped his arms around me. He pressed his head against my back and I more than welcomed it. I needed his warmth. I needed someone to hold me so I wouldn't fall apart.

"It's gonna be okay, baby. We'll get through this together." Arthur took in a deep breath.

"Okay. I love you."

"I love you too."

Things wouldn't be okay for a while, but it was a nice thing to say whenever something terrible happened. Perhaps it was the only thing you could say when your heart was being ripped out of your chest. Arthur was one of the few people in the world who could almost get me to feel like the world wasn't ending. Someone who understood me when all my dark, painful memories from the past stormed my mind all at once.

Aunt Vanya, Vera, and I wanted to pick out a plot of land at the cemetery to bury my mother. There was a gentle rustling of leaves as we wandered down a winding path, passing rows and rows of graves that extended across the vast grassy terrain. Headstones and monuments filled the landscape with a sense of solemn remembrance which caused me to drift through the various memories I had with my mother. Vanya held a bouquet of black roses to place down on our grandmother's headstone. We took advantage of the wind being light and breezy by sitting down on the ground to cool off. The sun was being blocked out by the clouds casting a greyish hue in the sky. It reflected how we felt.

"It still doesn't feel real." Vanya stared at the sky. She was still reeling from her sister's death. None of us felt like it was real. What made everything a 1000 times worse was how she died.

"Is it true someone broke into her house and killed her...with an axe?" Vera wiped away her tears. She had puffy circles around her eyes and her pupils were blood red. I felt for her. She was younger and had a better relationship with her. She felt horrible when she left to live with Vanya, but she knew she had to. My mother couldn't take care of her anymore. She could barely take care of herself.

"Chopped off her head and everything. Fuckin' savages took it too. They shouldn't have named this town St. Devil. They cursed it." Vanya nodded.

That's what the police had told us. Someone broke into her house the night of Caroline's funeral and murdered her with an axe. They knew by studying the markings on what was left of her neck. I didn't press for too many details. The storm masked any blood-curdling screams my mother might've let out. She never stood a chance. I had many questions regarding my mother's sudden, gruesome murder but one stood out to me the most. *Who could've done it and why?*

"Why do you guys think they killed mom?" I pondered aloud.

"Because people are really evil in this world." Vera stated.

"You're not wrong." I replied.

Vanya flipped her hair and rubbed two of her fingers together.

"Money. They killed her for money."

"The police said they didn't take anything from her house," I said.

"They must've missed something. Violet was rich. You know she was. Why else would anyone kill her? Do you think she had enemies?" Vanya asked.

"Mom didn't have enemies. She was rude to some people, but she barely even talked to anyone. She only talked to the neighbors sometimes. Walter Campbell and his wife, Sandra," Vera said.

"Walter Campbell huh?" I muttered.

"Your lover is here." Vanya grinned.

I turned and saw Arthur trudging up the hill towards us. I waved and he gave me a slight nod.

"He must be ecstatic that she's gone." Vanya whispered.

"Hey, don't say shit like that. It's not true." I snapped.

"Oh relax, he didn't hear me." Vanya shrugged.

"Hey guys. I'm sorry I'm late." Arthur sat down next to us.

"It's okay. You didn't miss anything. We're just being very sad together," Vanya said gently.

"I'll be sad with you guys." Arthur put his arm around me and pulled me in closer.

"What happened?" I asked.

"Well, I was out the door when two police officers randomly approached me. They asked me questions about Walter Campbell. Violet's old neighbor."

"The cops were at our house?" My heart jumped.

"Yeah but it's fine. They asked me a few questions then left."

"What happened with Walter?" Vanya poked her head forward, intently listening.

"Walter is apparently missing. Sandra Campbell reported it. That's his wife."

"What? That's really freaky," Vera said.

"You're kidding."

"Not at all. His car is missing too," Arthur added.

"Holy shit," I blurted out.

"What the hell?" Vanya echoed.

The same night that my mother had been murdered, Walter went missing along with his car. It was *very* strange. Things were about to get really bad. I sensed it back then and I was not wrong. Vanya squinted her eyes and looked through me.

"What?" I asked.

"Why is Dennis here?"

I turned around and saw a tall shadowy figure in the distance, staring. My Father's face was melancholic, and he nodded at me. I quickly turned back and felt a cold shiver trickle down my spine.

"Do we have to say hi to dad? I really don't want to." Vera whispered.

Vanya grabbed onto her hand and shook her head.

"I told him to stay away," I said coldly.

"He's never been one to listen," Vanya replied.

After everything he had done, my Father had no business being there. I wanted to kill him right then and there, but I knew he'd kill me first. He was a man of dark urges, and I knew he was hiding something. It would be revealed soon enough. I would make sure of it.

CHAPTER 3
PRESENT DAY

Arthur was on top of me, breathing heavily, thrusting back and forth as I wrapped my legs around him. We were in bed and had been going for about 7 minutes. He had gone a long way from the beginning of our relationship. I appreciated that. I wasn't into it at that current moment though and Arthur soon noticed. He stopped and rolled over.

"You're not here, are you?"

"I'm sorry, Arthur. I...my head's not in it. It's not you, I swear. It's me."

"I've heard that one before. Many, many times. Usually, it is me." Arthur dryly chuckled.

"It's not, trust me. You've improved a lot. I *swear*."

"Well, at least I can feel good about myself."

I was going to say it was my mother but that would've sounded weird out loud, even if it was true. Her murder was still affecting me greatly and my mind often drifted to visions of her head getting chopped off by an axe. It was horrifying and whenever that happened, it felt like a giant metal ring was stuck around my waist, becoming smaller and smaller, entrapping me, and strangling all the air out of me. That's what it felt like when Arthur was trying to put a child in me.

It felt like a trap. If I got pregnant I felt like that was it. There was no going back. I just wasn't sure if I wanted to bring a child into the world yet. I didn't think it would be fair to him or her. I knew I was going around in circles regarding the whole baby situation, but I didn't know what to do. There was too much going on in my head.

"Do you really wanna start a family?"

"I do. I swear to you that I do." I swung my hand onto his chest and rubbed it.

"I love you Venus, but my life feels incomplete. It's not that you're not enough, it's just...I feel like the time is now. I want to be a dad and want you to be the mother of our child. You still feel the same way, right?"

"Of course I do. I swear to you that we will have a family. I'm going to get through whatever I'm going through, and we will have a baby." I promised.

"Okay, I trust you. Have you thought about any names yet?"

"What about Victoria or Vanessa if it's a girl?"

"Does it have to start with a *V*?"

"Yes."

"Of course it does. I like Victoria."

"Me too."

Whether her name turned out to be Victoria, Vanessa, or Vladimir...I only hoped she lived for as long as possible. Being a girl in the Snow family was a curse.

While I was responding to feedback regarding my videos on Kenneth Kilhouser, I received an anonymous tip via email. There was a suspected double murder in a suburban house near me. I only got the location of the neighborhood so when I drove out there I kept my eyes peeled. I passed house after house after house. Nearly all of them had white picket fences and perfectly manicured lawns. It was like driving through a never-ending 1950s housewife-era nightmare world.

When I saw 7 police cruisers and emergency response vehicles parked near one house, I knew. I was so concentrated on trying to get a sneak peek for my followers that I hadn't even noticed who's house it was. I never once thought of the possibility. It would've never occurred to me in a 100 years. I got out my video camera and hit record. I saw the numbers *0905* and completely froze. A lump formed in my throat and an imaginary sharp knife plunged into my stomach. I dropped my camera on the floor mat of my car and started shaking. My breath was shallow, and I tightly gripped my steering wheel. I thought I was about to pass out when I saw paramedics bringing out two lifeless bodies on stretchers, covered in tarps. Before I knew it, I was flying through the cops who were running after me. I had broken through the yellow police tape and ignored their furious commands at me. I could barely even hear them since my ears sounded muffled. The only thing I heard was my heart pounding in my head. I stopped one paramedic dead in his tracks, and he flinched backwards, terrified. I unveiled the tarp for a few seconds and stared.

It was her.

Tears flowed out of my eyes and dripped down to the floor like pouring rain in a thunderstorm. I collapsed to the ground and started pulling blades of grass out. I was screaming like a wild animal and bawling like someone was stabbing me to death. The police were trying to escort me away, but I stayed put. I allowed my grief to overcome any motor functions I may have still possessed at that time. Seeing her little, skinny body like that was enough to shatter my heart into a million, tiny pieces. I would never be the same ever again. I kept screaming the same thing over and over.

Where is her head?!

Where is her head?!

WHERE IS HER HEAD?!

Vera's head. It was gone. Just like my mother's. A sick, twisted, deranged bastard had murdered my little sister and took her head. I didn't even have to uncover the other body. It was my Aunt Vanya. She had been murdered too, just like that. I didn't understand any of it and I wasn't even sure if I wanted to at that time. But the truth was, I had no choice. I needed to find the monster responsible for slaughtering my entire family. My mother, my aunt, and my little sister. Who was next?

Arthur eventually came and I vaguely remember him taking me off the front lawn of Aunt Vanya's house. We sat down on a curb near our cars, and he held me as tight as he could.

"Vanya and Vera?" Arthur whispered as low as possible.

"Yeah," I sobbed.

Arthur cried and stroked my hair to comfort me. That was all he needed to know. We stayed awake for several hours the day of their murders. We laid down together on the sofa at home and in bed. We didn't say a single word to each other. Arthur knew that what I needed was to know that I was not alone. I needed to cry and grieve while he was near me. I was very vulnerable, and he knew that.

The next month was an utter whirlwind as I dealt with the belongings of Vanya's house and the ensuing funeral services. Thankfully my Father paid for them both without me asking. We held it in a funeral home with closed caskets. Nobody wanted to see 2 headless corpses through a glass display, me included. That one time was more than enough for the rest of my life. While I remained socially dormant in a couch chair in a dark corner of the viewing room, my Father shamelessly mingled with everyone who entered and accepted their condolences with a superficial sadness glossed over his face. I knew the truth. The truth that no one wanted to accept. Father wasn't sad that they were gone. I felt it in my bones. It permeated throughout my body like a vicious infection. He was wearing a mask that hid who he truly was. I planned to uncover it.

Arthur was doing me the favor of receiving family and friends who knew me personally. I had a stormy cloud hanging over my head. I didn't want to utter a single breath to anyone that day. I knew people would understand. My entire family had been ripped apart in less than a year. The last thing I ever expected to happen...happened. I decided right then and there that I couldn't have a child. I couldn't bring myself to have a baby in a world where their grandmother, their great aunt and their aunt were gone. Three loved ones butchered and senselessly murdered. A world without my mother, Aunt Vanya and Vera wasn't a world my baby was going to grow up in. I promised myself I would consider getting an abortion if I ever did end up getting pregnant. I wouldn't tell Arthur. I couldn't. I hated myself for even thinking that, but I was dealing with some very tragic circumstances. There was no guide on how to live life and happily move on after 3 of your closest family members are slaughtered like animals by a cruel psychopath. I was alone. No one knew how I felt. No one could relate. I was the only one. I was a viral news story. I was a cautionary tale. I was a true crime poster girl, and it angered me to my core.

Once my Father was done speaking with Sandra Campbell, Walter's wife, he drifted over to me. My heart sank and I held my guard up. I was definitely not in the mood.

"Hey sweetheart. How are you doing?"

"I'm fine."

"Okay. I can't believe any of this, you know? First my own brother died. Poor David. Bless him. Violet was killed by some lunatic and now this. Your Aunt Vanya and our little Vera are dead. The police have no breakthroughs in Violet's investigation and now they have two more victims. We need to brace ourselves, Venus. I don't think we'll have the answers we want for a long, long time." Father explained.

"I don't want to talk about it, dad."

"I'm sorry. I get it. Our family is going through a great deal of suffering at the moment, but things will get better. They have to. Just give it time."

I almost believed him. My Father had a way with words. He knew how to inspire...and how to instill fear.

"Why were you talking to Sandra?"

"Oh, Walter's still missing. She asked me about him. She's very desperate to find him but at this point...who knows if he's still...you know." Father raised his eyebrows.

After my mother's murder, Walter had gone missing. Nearly a year later, he was still missing and there was no real trace of him. I heard the police investigated a couple of leads they had but they went cold. The case was open and up in the air. Who knew what the hell was going on in St. Devil.

"I see. More dead people probably."

"Hey, you know I love you right? I loved Violet and Vera too. I promise you. Okay?" Father stared deep into my soul. I shrugged him off.

"Okay dad," I mumbled.

He walked away and started charming everyone again. If only they knew what he really was.

For the next few weeks after the murders, I mainly stayed in bed. I would drag myself out of my sheets in the mornings to go for a brisk jog and then it was back under the covers. I spent my hours traversing the internet on my tablet, reading through every theory and article I could find relating to my family's murders. They already had a name. The *St. Devil Beheadings.*

"THREE WOMEN SLAIN. ONE SUSPECTED SERIAL KILLER."

That was the headline of one article I read. People believed that a serial killer murdered my family. I didn't disagree. The method of murder was the same for all three. The killer would murder them with an axe and then chop off their heads to possibly add to some sort of depraved trophy collection. They had found a bloodied axe at Aunt Vanya's house. It looked like the one my Father used when I was little. I never forgot that axe.

The article mentioned that I could be next. Seeing the name *Venus Duarte* made my skin crawl and my stomach flare. I rocketed my tablet across the room, in a sudden fit of rage. I was beyond pissed. Why did some sick *fucker* feel the need to slaughter *my* family and why did I have to be next? It was complete bullshit. I didn't want to end up on a true crime documentary. I watched them. I didn't feature on them as a dead woman, tragically ripped to shreds by some rampaging psychopath. I reported on true crime. That was supposed to be the extent of my involvement.

I went outside to think and sat on my tire swing. How could I have kept my promise? It wasn't possible. Not after everything that happened.

Monsters never win. If only that were true.

When I woke up in the morning and when I went to sleep at night all I thought about was them. Mom, Aunt, Sister. Violet, Vanya, Vera. All murdered, dead, and gone forever. I would never celebrate another birthday or holiday with my family ever again. My mother would never become a grandmother. I couldn't laugh at Aunt Vanya's jokes anymore. My sister would never get to take care of her nephew or niece. She never even got the chance to experience life beyond her young adult years. She never truly got to fall in love with a good man and she never got to discover her true passion in life. I would never play *Parcheesi* with my little sister ever again. Vera's death hit the hardest. The youngest ones always did.

I heard a harsh crunch next door. I stood up and peeked over to the neighbor's backyard. A man was chopping wooden blocks with an axe. I quickly crouched down and grew dizzy. I got a hot flash and remembered that my Father had an axe in his garage. The same weapon that was used to kill my family. I repressed many memories from my childhood on purpose. I didn't like the fact that I needed to delve deep and dig them out to find the truth behind the killings. It didn't matter. I needed to know who the serial killer was, and I needed to know *why*. Why did he or she take my family away from me?

As I allowed my own thoughts to consume me. One name kept popping up in my head.

Dennis Snow.

Could my own Father be a serial killer?

I couldn't cross him off the list. He was hiding something. That much I knew.

CHAPTER 4

I didn't plan on dying. I had things to do and a life to live. I had to live on for them. But I couldn't begin to move on just yet. I was hellbent on finding the serial killer. I wouldn't rest until I knew who he was and until he was erased. I refused to be murdered. That asshole was not going to slice my head off. I flipped the camera on my phone and sat down on the edge of my bed. I pressed record to send an important video to all of my followers.

"Hi everyone. By now you probably know what happened to me. If you don't, a terrible tragedy happened to my family. An alleged serial killer murdered my Aunt Vanya and my little sister, Vera. You all know my mother was murdered many months ago and they never found the killer. Well, the internet believes that the same killer who murdered my mom has struck again. I am inclined to believe it. That's why I'm going on an indefinite hiatus. I need to find this serial killer, solve the mystery, and eventually reveal the whole truth behind these tragic slayings. You have all helped me in the past. You helped me catch one serial killer, Kenneth Kilhouser. Maybe you can help me catch another one. One who is an immediate threat to my own life. Anonymous tips are more than welcome and appreciated. Thank you all. I hope to talk to you soon."

I stopped the recording and uploaded it to all of my social media platforms. I put my phone face down on the bed and rubbed my aching eyes. I hadn't slept much at all since the murders. Whenever I closed my eyes, all I saw were headless bodies. It was enough to make me vomit. Arthur came to the door and knocked. I nodded and he came in to sit with me.

"You're done?"

"Just finished."

"I think your fans are gonna miss you." He put his arm around my waist.

"I think so too but duty calls."

"Right. I've been meaning to talk to you about that."

"What's wrong?" I sensed it in his voice.

"I don't think it's a good idea to hunt down the person responsible for murdering your family. I mean, he's a serial killer. That's insane. It's dangerous." Arthur's eyes were full of concern.

"I know it is, but I have to do this. I don't want to be fucking next, Arthur. Do you?" I warned.

Arthur pulled me in tighter and caressed my cheek.

"Don't even say that. You will *not* be next. You're going to live. You're going to live for them," Arthur stressed.

"I won't be able to live for anyone if he's still out there."

"What if you try to find him while staying here at home? I'll hire a private security guard or something. Someone who'll watch the house 24/7."

"I have to go out, Arthur. I have to visit locations, search for clues and question people. It's the only way I'll find this asshole."

"Okay, let's say you do find him. What then? What are you gonna do? Shoot him?"

"I'll let the police know and I'll hand over the evidence that would incriminate him as the killer. It would be the same process I did with Kilhouser." I explained.

"What if he catches on to you first and kills you? I mean, you already announced online that you intend to catch him. I'm willing to bet he watched that video."

"That's not very likely."

"But, it is likely."

"I'm doing this, babe. I'm sorry if you're worried about me, but you don't need to be. I can handle myself. I've done it before, and I can do it again. Kilhouser's dead, remember?"

"I love to be reminded of that." Arthur rolled his eyes.

"It's gonna be okay. I promise." I held his hand and squeezed.

I really had no idea if things were going to be okay. But I had to lie to appease him. I needed him calm to let me do my thing. I couldn't relax knowing that psycho was still out there. I needed him in prison, or preferably— dead. Only then would I be at peace.

"Well, alright. If you say so."

"Thank you." I kissed him on the cheek.

"Also, we can obviously hold off on having a baby for now. We're going through something tremendously painful, and I don't need you stressing over it."

"I appreciate that."

Arthur went back to work, defeated. I knew he was keeping up appearances. He was worried because I was searching for a mysterious serial killer and the whole baby thing was out of the question for the time being. I felt for my husband. I really did. If anyone deserved a happy ending, it was him.

I went into the bathroom and remembered the first time; Arthur and I had sex. He had accidentally finished in me and was freaking out.

Oh my god the condom broke. I swear I didn't do it on purpose.

I'm so sorry. I swear I didn't mean to.

I'll do anything. I'll get a job if you're pregnant. I'll devote my life to our baby.

I'll take care of you. I'll never leave you. I promise.

I love you so much, Venus.

He was being silly of course, but very sweet. I told him about the magic of the morning-after pill, and he calmed down. He was about to have a full-blown panic attack. I was worried he would pass out. That's the type of man, Arthur was. If it weren't for him I probably would have done something drastic to myself. I had a history, unfortunately.

Before I embarked on my mission, I decided to take a pregnancy test. A precautionary measure to ensure I wasn't pregnant already. I highly doubted it, but I needed to be sure. It was a good thing I did it too. The test came out positive. The absolute last thing I needed. I couldn't believe I was already pregnant. Arthur's seed turned out to be very potent or I was more prone to pregnancy than I imagined. Whatever the case was, I had a big problem on my hands.

"Fuck me," I muttered aloud.

I stayed in there for a good hour, thinking about what to do. I couldn't tell Arthur. He'd go crazy. He'd never let me leave the house. He'd lock me in a cage if he could. No way. I couldn't risk going to an OB/GYN either. Someone would definitely spot me and recognize me. My face had been plastered all over the local news.

VENUS DUARTE PREGNANT. A PRIME TARGET FOR THE TWISTED SERIAL KILLER WHO KILLED HER FAMILY.

I already saw the headlines. *Fuck no*. I thought about the abortion but decided against it. I rubbed my belly and actually smiled. The first time I had smiled in a very long time. A baby. My baby. He or she was actually growing inside of me. I knew then that I had no choice. I had to stop the serial killer no matter what. It meant life or death for not only me but my baby. I took a deep breath and wiped the tears that were streaming down my face.

I decided to make a pact with myself. I would only have the baby if I was able to find the serial killer and put him away for an eternity. That meant that I had a few weeks until I *showed* to find the killer. If I didn't find him by then, I would gladly die with my baby. It sounded absolutely horrific, but I knew I was next. I felt it in my bones. I felt deathly sick at the thought of Arthur losing me...his pregnant wife, but I couldn't live my life in fear or regret. I refused to raise my baby if I was unable to complete what I needed to do. The most important thing I would ever do in my entire life. My survival and my future family's survival depended solely on me.

My pregnant belly would apparently show in 12 to 18 weeks. That was my exact timeframe for finding the truth. I'd have to hide my pregnancy symptoms and cope for the time being. I knew it was dangerous not to see a medical professional, but I needed it to be a secret for the time being. I couldn't risk it. I would hold out for as long as possible unless it was absolutely necessary to check things out.

Unexpectedly, my Father invited me and Arthur to his lakehouse. He wanted to fish with him. I reluctantly accepted. We took the long winding road to his house. It was a scenic route. There was nothing but greenery and great grass fields on opposite sides of the road. We passed by a massive farm that had cows, chickens, horses, and goats. My Father loved the countryside. He secretly liked being alone in the wilderness. I always wondered why.

Arthur hated my Father more than my mother, but I still didn't want to tell him about my theory. The theory that he could potentially be a serial killer. He'd most likely laugh in my face and have me committed to a psychiatric facility.

"Are you sure you want to visit him?" Arthur asked.

"I don't but he's the only family I got left. I know I'm not obligated but once a year doesn't hurt I guess. Just to make sure I get that monthly inheritance check."

And I need to go through his things to see if he has that axe.

"I'm surprised you call him family after all the shit he did to you."

"It's in the past."

"If you say so. Do I have to fish with him?"

"Maybe for a couple of hours at most," I replied.

"That'll be fun." Arthur groaned.

When we arrived, we parked near the shimmering lake. My Father's lakehouse was built with a combination of wood, stone, and brick. It was a rustic, earthy residence that was handcrafted with the finest materials money could buy. It had large windows, a fully furnished interior living room and a patio that included a gas-powered fireplace along with an outdoor kitchen. It was yet another reminder that my Father was a very wealthy man who lived for the finer things in life...or so he said.

He was waiting for us outside and smiling as we walked towards him. He firmly shook Arthur's hand and gave me a hug. I made sure to quickly pull away.

"I'm really glad you guys came to visit me. I wanted to see you both after the deaths of Vanya and my little Vera." Father swallowed hard.

"How could we turn you down?"

"I appreciate that, Arthur. I don't think Venus would've came here on her own." Father smirked.

"You are correct." I snapped.

"Hey, c'mon, let's not fight. I'm sorry. I wasn't trying to start anything. You and I are the only ones left, Venus. Violet, Vanya, Vera and...David are all gone."

I sighed and nodded.

"Can we go inside please? It's hot," I said.

"Oh goodness, of course. Where are my manners? Let's go inside and get some refreshments." Father motioned for us to follow him.

I snuck a look at Arthur and put a pretend gun to my head. He smirked and shook his head. When we got inside, I was awe-struck. He had updated the place. It was a lot nicer than before. The wooden floor had been repolished and was glossy. The furniture was modern, and he had a rectangular, built-in display case for his hunting rifle which was installed above the main fireplace. It was a Lee-Enfield. An 1895 bolt-action repeating rifle that he had proudly bought at a gun convention. I hated that thing. He used to threaten me with it whenever we'd visit the lakehouse. He used to get so angry back then. He got better at hiding it as I got older, but I knew he was still the same violent man with a hair-trigger temper.

My Father served us glasses of ice-cold lemonade and told us to sit down at his dinner table. He had cooked for us. Arthur was giddy.

"Why are you acting like that?" I asked.

"This means I don't have to go fishing. It's getting dark out and we're about to eat."

"He likes to go at night too. There's this thing called *night fishing*. It's where you fish at night," I replied.

"I never would've guessed."

"You really don't wanna go huh?"

"It's fine. I will deal with it."

"You don't have to do it. I can make something up."

"No, it's okay. I'll do it for you." Arthur grabbed my hand and ran his thumb across my palm. He let go when my Father walked in with a large platter of mashed potatoes, seasoned chicken cutlets and a Roma tomato salad. He served us heaping portions then sat down. My Father always knew how to make someone feel invited. He knew how to talk to people and how to make them feel important. It's how he was able to snag my mother. A very picky, uppity woman who rejected him twice. My mother eventually accepted when my Father hired a classical music band to play outside her house until she said yes to one date. She was impressed at his persistence and realized he wasn't like the other boys. That became truer as the years went on in the most sinister way possible. She had no idea what she had gotten herself into. The most dangerous forms of abuse are the ones that are hidden behind a thin veil of love and compassion. Unfortunately, my mother learned that the hard way.

"Venus, have the detectives talked to you about Vanya and Vera yet?" Father asked.

"They did. They asked me where I was and if I knew anything. I knew nothing obviously. Same deal with mom. I knew jack shit."

"They talked to me too. This whole thing is a mystery. I was in the office when I got the call. I was a mess. I could barely breathe."

"We should talk about something else," I said forcefully.

I didn't like to think about Aunt Vanya's and Vera's heads being sliced off their bodies. Especially when I was eating.

"This is a great dinner, Dennis. Thank you," Arthur complimented.

"You're very welcome. I don't get to cook much for other people. I don't get many guests these days," Father said.

"No one from business?" Arthur asked.

"All they wanna do is pitch me. I tell them to fuck off. I'm too old for that shit. I don't mind being alone. It's peaceful."

"No secret lovers? I find that hard to believe," I said skeptically.

"I'm a little too old for those exciting rendezvouses, sweetheart. I like to focus on my businesses and enjoy the outdoors."

My Father was many things, but he was loyal to my mom. I never heard any rumors of cheating surrounding him ever. My mother never mentioned that either. He never went out with other women unless it was mom. That was all fine and dandy until he started hitting her.

"What do you do outdoors?" I asked.

"I like to fish; I like to hunt..." Father trailed.

"Have you hunted anything lately?"

"No."

"What about deer?" Arthur asked.

What about people?

"I said no." Father was staring down at his plate with a stern face.

I crossed my arms and analyzed him. He had grown annoyed at the subject and was trying to find an out. I knew him all too well.

"Does your dad cook, Arthur?" Father asked.

"Dad!" I made a cutthroat gesture. I had no idea why he was bringing up Arthur's family.

"What?" Father shrugged.

"It's okay, Venus. It's just—, my dad wasn't around much. He liked to drink and bet at sports bars almost every single night. My dad cooking? Not in a million years." Arthur chuckled.

"Oh, I'm very sorry to hear that. I didn't know," Father said.

"You never asked," I snapped.

"It's okay. That part of my life has been mostly over for a long time now." Arthur touched my thigh to try and ease me.

"Your mother cooked for you then," Father stated.

"Can we stop with the interrogation please?" I rubbed Arthur's back. I knew it was a touchy subject for him. He didn't like to talk about that, ever. That's why my Father never even knew about Arthur's family issues until that night at the lakehouse.

"My mother was depressed for a long time, Dennis. She overdosed on pills when I was young. I was mostly raised by an aunt, my mother's sister." Arthur stared into space, reminiscing about the dark times in his life.

"I know what it's like to lose loved ones. Obviously. I understand your pain. I feel it. You can always lean on me for support, Arthur. You too, Venus. I'm here for you both. What's left of my beautiful family." Father choked up.

"We appreciate that." I secretly rolled my eyes.

"I remember Vera when she was younger. She would climb out of her crib when she was a baby and she found it so funny when I caught her. She'd look up at me, smile and laugh. It was the most adorable thing ever. I miss her so much."

"I do too," I whispered.

"Oh and Vanya. What a funny woman she was. I miss her presence. She was one hell of a drinker that one. She might've rivaled your daddy." Father chuckled.

"Do you like saying things out loud that you're not supposed to say out loud?" I asked.

"This one always likes to talk in riddles. We're gonna go fishing now. You can have your lonely woman time now." Father looked at Arthur who was getting up.

"I will be enjoying my lonely woman time. Thank you."

"I'll see you later baby." Arthur kissed the top of my head and followed him outside.

"Let me tell you something I've learned about all women…" Father rambled on.

Once they were out of sight, I began searching and rummaging through everything. If my Father murdered the women, there was bound to be some sort of proof somewhere. I went and looked in every kitchen cabinet, drawer, crevice, crack, and waste basket. I found nothing. Unfortunately, my Father was a very capable and intelligent person. He was gonna be hard to investigate. As I searched through the back, I found a door with a lock on it that needed a key. My heart began to pound.

Why does dad have a locked door in his lakehouse? What is he hiding there?

I needed to open it. I ran around the house looking for a hammer or a heavy mallet. Anything that could break the lock. I went to the display case for the hunting rifle and considered it. I couldn't do it. If I got it and used it to find evidence that my Father killed my family, he'd be next, and I wouldn't be able to restrain myself from shooting him. As tempting as that sounded, I loved my husband, and I had our future child growing inside of me. I needed to be careful. I couldn't risk it. It was also possible he'd hear the glass break and then all hell would break loose.

No. I need to be smart about this. He's a powerful man with a lot of important officials in his circles. I'm the outlier here. I have no backup. I screw up once...I can end up dead. Game over.

I went outside and searched through his patio. Fortunately, I found a very heavy rock. I picked it up and stuffed it inside my pocket. Before I went back inside, I glanced at the lake from a distance and saw that the boys were indeed fishing. Arthur seemed bored out of his mind as my Father battered him with his relentless conversation.

It's for a good cause. I love you.

I went to the locked door and started hitting the shit out of the lock with the rock. After about 20 tries, it finally broke and clicked open. I slid it off the handle and let it hit the floor with a massive *thud*. I slowly turned the knob on the door and pushed. When I stepped in, my insides convulsed, and I began to breathe rapidly. I tried to calm myself down by closing my eyes and remembering the time I took Vera out to the mall to get makeovers. She was so happy then. I was too. She always wanted to get ice cream afterwards and I always made sure we did. Even if I was down to my last few dollars. I wanted her to forget about our parents constantly arguing. I wanted her to forget about our Father's weekly storms of violence. It was beginning to seriously weigh down on her. I could tell. But it didn't matter anymore. She was gone. In the end...I hadn't done enough. I had failed her.

When I opened my eyes, everything was still there. It wasn't a nightmare after all. Nearly every inch of that room was covered with hung pictures and portraits of David Snow. My uncle. My Father's younger brother. The one who hung himself. It was a shrine to him. A disturbing one.

Many of them were of Uncle David with my Father when they were younger. When they played in the snow, when they first rode bikes, when they went to their high school proms and when David was the best man at my Father's wedding. There was even a hand-drawn portrait of David where he was an elderly man. It was the most bizarre thing I had ever seen. I made sure to lock the door behind me just in case they came back. I wasn't done looking. Below the weird, elderly fake David portrait was a wooden chest. It had no lock and an easy enough latch to open. The perfect place to hide an axe. The alleged murder weapon used to decapitate my family.

It was also big enough to hold a human head or a few. I knew I was mentally disturbed when that was the first thought that popped into my head when I saw it.

I slowly inched my way towards the chest, squatted down and placed my hand on the latch. Just then, I heard commotion outside. I quickly sprang up and bolted towards the door. I put my hand on the doorknob, but I didn't want to turn it. I didn't want to go. I wanted answers. I wanted to know what was inside that chest. The one my Father was trying to hide from the world. After they began calling out my name, it didn't take long for them to find where I was.

"Venus, why is there a broken lock on the floor?" Father asked.

"Oh shit," Arthur said aloud.

I heard a monstrous stomping towards the door that made the whole room shake, so I backed away. A ferocious pounding followed at the door as I heard Arthur trying to calm him down.

"What the hell are you doing in there?! Get out! Get out now!" Father shouted.

"Why does this exist?!" I shot back.

"It's none of your business! It's private!"

"I deserve to know why!"

"Why the fuck do you think you deserve to know anything?!

"Because I'm your daughter! The only one left!"

There was silence. The pounding stopped. It was almost like I could hear my Father thinking. After what seemed like hours, I decided to swing open the door. Father and Arthur were startled. Arthur even more so once he saw what was inside.

"What the hell..." Arthur mumbled as he stepped back.

I backed up and raised my arms, questioning the very existence of that room. Father quietly stepped forward and gazed around the room. He grinned to himself and scoffed.

"I haven't been here in a long time." Father rubbed his eyebrows.

"Dad, what is this? This is...this is weird shit."

"I loved your uncle, you know that. It destroyed me when he died. My life was never the same after that. I wanted somewhere where I could remember him in peace and where I could relive all the happy memories I had with him. I know it looks strange but...to me it isn't. It's my love for him. Growing up, we only had each other. I was supposed to protect him...I failed." Father said.

He was unflinching when he spoke. He drew you in with the soft intensity of his eyes and his booming, baritone voice. I almost believed him. I knew Arthur did. But no one knew him like I did. I knew that David's death wrecked him to his core when it happened. It changed him for the worst...and he took it all out on us.

"I'm sorry about your brother, Dennis," Arthur offered.

"Thank you son."

I wanted to puke all over the floor, but I understood. Nearly everyone fell for my Father's charm. He would've made an exemplary cult leader. Well, for all I knew he could've already been in one. Rich people always did weird shit like that.

"What's in the chest?" I commanded.

"You didn't take a look inside?" Father asked.

"No, I didn't. Does that worry you?"

"Not really no. Take a look. You already broke the place down." Father smirked.

I took him up on his offer and went to the chest. I wasted no time. As it creaked open, I closed my eyes for a brief moment. When I looked, I saw nothing. I slowly placed my hand inside and felt around the entire chest until I felt a slippery substance. I grabbed onto it and raised it up so I could see. It was a yellow piece of notebook paper. There was something scrawled in black ink.

"I'm so sorry, but I had to do it. I hated you all."

I gasped and placed my hand over my mouth. I had never seen that note before in my life. My Father had never mentioned its existence.

"Dad, what the hell is this?"

"It's a suicide note," Father practically whispered.

"Jesus Christ," Arthur said softly.

"Did anyone else know he left one?" I asked.

"No. I never told anyone. It's a horrible thing to leave behind, Venus," Father said.

"He really hated all of us."

"No, I don't believe that. I don't know what happened exactly, but David didn't hate *all* of us. I know he didn't hate me."

It was true. Uncle David worshipped my Father. The note didn't make any sense. From what I remembered, he hated Aunt Vanya and my mother. An accumulation of arguments and altercations that spiraled into a full-blown grudge between the three of them. I turned the paper around and saw something else. **505-555-0005.**

"There's a phone number here. What is this?"

"To this day, I'm not sure. You wouldn't believe the trouble I went through trying to find who owned that phone number. I looked online, I combed through city phone records and ended up talking to over 40 people. They had no idea who David was, or they were all lying."

"I'm assuming you called it, and no one answered," I said.

"Worse, it was out of service. To this day I believe the answer to David's death lies in that phone number, but I stopped looking. It nearly drove me insane."

My Father bent down and picked up a white envelope that had been taped to the side of the chest.

"What's that?" I asked.

"It's a letter I began writing to David, many years ago. I never finished it. It was too painful. I think I'll finish it now." He stuffed it inside his pocket.

"So you have no idea who it could've been? Maybe an ex-girlfriend or someone he shouldn't have been speaking with?" Arthur asked.

"After his wife died, he no longer wanted any romantic relationships. He was done with that. The police had a wild theory, but the more I thought about it the more I thought it was viable. I could be crazy, but at this point I'd believe anything."

"What was it?" I took out my phone and copied the phone number down.

"They think the phone number belonged to a hitman that David hired to kill someone. David might've changed his mind and that's when things went downhill." Father explained.

I couldn't imagine Uncle David hiring a *hitman* of all things to kill anyone. But stranger things have happened. He was mild-mannered for the most part, but he had said things in the past that made you question what lurked in the quiet corners of his mind. He was my Father's brother after all.

"You can't believe that. That's insane."

"At this point, I don't know. I've had hundreds of sleepless nights going over it in my head. David really hated Violet and Vanya. Maybe one night he decided to act on it, regretted it and couldn't live with the guilt." Father sighed.

"If there was a hitman he never went through with it, right?" Arthur inquired.

"No. He or she didn't. At least I don't think so. David died years ago. These murders were very recent. I don't know what to think anymore. Another theory is that he hired a hitman to kill *him* because he was depressed or some bullshit. Like I said, I don't know what to think anymore."

I did. I was going to find out who that phone number belonged to. I didn't know how or why, but David's suicide seemed connected to the *St. Devil Beheadings*. I was going to find out what really happened.

CHAPTER 5
15 YEARS EARLIER

I tried to remember everything I could about Uncle David. I had a memory of a family Christmas party he attended when I was in college. I was having my first Christmas with Arthur. My parents, Uncle David, Aunt Vanya, Vera, Barry, and Caroline were all there. They were all alive at that time. It was hard to think about.

The party was at my parent's house. A colossal two-story home with a spacious living room, a fully stocked kitchen and a warm, inviting atmosphere that quickly dissipated once the arguments started. It was ironic hearing cursing and screaming amidst the backdrop of *"Jingle Bell, Jingle Bell, Jingle Bell...Rock."*

Arthur and I were sitting on the couch together near the massive, heavily decorated Christmas tree. Aunt Vanya was with us and drinking as she usually did. Her wide frame caused our bodies to be squished together but we didn't mind. We loved being with her. She was that stereotypical cool aunt who you always felt good about. My Father didn't pay much mind to Arthur. He didn't hate him, and we had no way of telling if he liked him. I was just grateful he didn't give him any trouble considering how he was. My mother on the other hand was insufferable. She examined his every move, critiqued all his clothing, and questioned his ability to provide for me as a future husband. I would get into shouting matches with her over him and I had to remind myself at the end of the day that my mother was only doing it out of love. She was married to a monster, and she didn't want me to make the same grave, life-ending mistake. That's the story I told myself anyway.

"Your mother's coming over here. She doesn't look happy." Arthur nudged me.

"That's how she usually looks." I snickered.

"Why are you so close to her?" My mother asked him.

"Oh, sorry Miss Snow. It's because of Vanya. It's a small couch," Arthur said.

Vanya threw back her head in uproarious laughter. Mother was not amused one bit.

"Are you suggesting my sister is too wide?" She scowled.

"Oh leave him alone. He's not suggesting anything. It's true." Vanya giggled.

"Don't talk about yourself like that. It's humiliating. You're a lady." She raised her pointy chin.

"No shit," Vanya replied.

"You're a disgrace." My mother grimaced and turned heel.

"See Arthur? I told you. I always have a good time with my lovely sister on Christmas."

"I noticed," Arthur answered.

"Well, we have that to look forward to for the rest of our lives."

"We could move out of the country," Arthur suggested.

"I'm game. Let's move...to literally anywhere else on this planet. I wouldn't mind moving to the Sun, but we'd burn up and die," I said.

"It would also take us like a whole year to get there," Arthur stated.

"Shut up nerd."

"What? It's true."

"Well, at least we wouldn't have to talk to my Mother anymore," I said quietly.

"That's better than winning the lottery."

We laughed as my Mother glanced at us. She had a stern expression on her face. When she looked away I saw her face soften. She seemed to smile. It lasted just a few seconds as she noticed everyone having a good time. She even mouthed a few words to the Christmas song playing. My Mother wasn't evil, but it was easy to think that she was. Most of her good deeds were done behind closed doors. She organized the entire party herself and decorated everything, including the gorgeous Christmas tree. She sent out all the invites and cooked all the food. Vera and I helped her somewhat and for a time she was at peace. We even enjoyed helping her. For once I felt a familiar warmth in my heart. That was all shattered when my Father saw how much she had spent. They had a massive argument and the good times quickly ended. My Mother finished doing the rest of the work while my Father stormed away to his business office to "cool off".

When she was still alive I asked my Mother about the incident, and she refused to acknowledge that it had happened. She denied its existence. She told me it was all in my head. That was why I had trouble discerning reality from fiction when it came to my memories.

That's why I tried to bury all the bad memories I had deep in my mind. I'd remember something but then my Mother, my Father or my Aunt Vanya would tell me it wasn't real or true. It almost made me go insane. My Mother would tell me that the abuse I sustained at the hands of my Father wasn't exactly accurate and that as a child I had exaggerated the things that I had experienced. That enraged me. I knew what I felt. I knew what had happened. But she made me doubt everything because I had been a kid. All she'd tell me was that things were very complicated throughout my childhood.

That's what adults tell you when they don't want you to know the truth. They want to hide the fact that they gave you everlasting trauma. They don't want to accept the consequences of what they did to their own children. Their desire to feel innocent outweighs their guilt.

"What about moving to Venus? It's my name. Everyone says Mars, but why not a planet with my name?"

"That's not a bad idea," Arthur said.

"Yes it is! You're not going anywhere. I'll have you arrested," Vanya threatened.

"On what charge?" I asked.

"For reckless abandonment of your aunty."

"I don't think that applies in that situation," Arthur said.

"I don't think you apply to anything, *Arnold*." Vanya playfully slapped his arm.

"That's not my name." Arthur chuckled.

Vanya ignored him and downed her drink.

"Hmm. I need another," Vanya mumbled.

Uncle David was playing *Parcheesi* with Vera on the kitchen counter. He beamed whenever they spent time together. Out of everyone in the family I believed that David only truly loved Vera and his brother. I loved her too. She made it easy. She was a sweet, innocent girl. I liked to call her my shining star. She loved the way that sounded. David almost had a daughter once, but his wife had a miscarriage. He never talked about it and neither did my Father. Vera must've reminded him of the daughter he never had.

Vanya drunkenly stood up and stumbled forward. Arthur sprang up to hold her, but Vanya swatted his hands away.

"Sorry I thought you were gonna fall."

"Hands off the merchandise, pervert." Vanya glanced back and winked.

"Did that just happen?" Arthur sat back down.

"I told you. She has a weird sense of humor."

Vanya strolled towards David and Vera. She started touching the *Parcheesi* board which annoyed David so much his eye started twitching.

"How are you liking the game, sweetie pie?" Vanya asked.

"It's really fun. I like playing with Uncle David," Vera said.

"Oh yeah? I bet it would be even more fun to play with Aunt Vanya."

"Yay!" Vera cheered.

"Get away from here." David mouthed.

Vanya shook her head and took a seat on an empty barstool.

"We can all have fun together." Vanya smiled.

"Right. Of course." David forced a grin.

"Your uncle looks like he's about to implode. He's normally relaxed." Arthur observed.

"Yeah, he's pissed. The Aunt Vanya effect."

"Should we do something?" Arthur asked.

"Nope. He'll get over it. Listen, I'm gonna see if we can sneak out of here for a couple of hours. I'm bored. Let me go find my parents. If I don't say anything, I won't hear the fucking end of it."

"Yeah, sure. I'll wait here."

I kissed him on the cheek and got up to search for my Mother. If I told her I knew the message would get to my Father eventually. I knew he didn't like to be interrupted at public events and parties. He was prideful and loved being the center of attention. He told never-ending stories and life lessons about his business and his family's history. It was utterly nauseating.

I found my parents along with Barry and Caroline in the wide hallway that connected the living room and the kitchen. They watched in silent, collective horror as my Mother argued with my Father. I froze and cringed as my Father tried to wave her off.

"You need to tell Vera to go pick up her room. It's a mess!"

"Violet, she's playing with her uncle. What the hell is the problem? It's Christmas!" Father boomed.

"She needs to clean it. It's been a mess for days," Mother demanded.

"Then go tell her."

"I already did. She won't listen."

"I'm sure she'll do it later. Please stop with this idiotic nonsense. I'm talking with our guests. You're embarrassing us!" He practically shook the walls because of how loud he shouted.

I trembled as I turned my head away, all the feelings from when I was younger bubbling up in my stomach.

"You're a fucking egomaniac." Mother snapped.

"I'm a fucking egomaniac who makes all the money and pays all the bills."

Violet marched away from him and brushed past me as my Father continued on with his conversation like nothing happened. That's how normal it was for him. That's how I knew something wasn't right in his head.

"Anyway, after I invested with the Dutch Brothers I quadrupled their annual revenue and provided them with resources that allowed them to open 4 more farms. Obviously I own a good chunk of their company and I was able to acquire some scenic properties for my own uses." Father sipped his mug of hot chocolate as Barry and Caroline awkwardly smiled and nodded. They were still processing the explosive argument they had just witnessed while my Father had already moved on.

When I turned to see what my Mother was doing, I saw her yank the *Parcheesi* game away from Vera and Uncle David. She launched it across the room, and it crashed against a cupboard in the kitchen. The pieces spilled all over the floor and made a huge mess. Vera began to cry as Uncle David's face twisted with absolute rage. I had never seen him like that before that day. Vanya quickly sobered up and jumped off her chair. The entire house grew silent as my Mother began her tirade.

"Go clean your room now or no presents!" Mother commanded.

Vera ran away screaming and crying. I tried to grab her, but she zoomed past me and slammed her door shut. Everyone was shocked. Father glared at my Mother and rubbed his eyes in frustration.

"Violet, it's Christmas! What the hell is the matter with you?" Vanya asked.

"She needs to obey my commands when I give them," Mother said.

"What is she? Your foot soldier? It is Christmas. There was no need for any of that. What the hell possessed you to grab our game and destroy it? That was horribly violent and disrespectful. Are you a demon?" David asked.

"She's my daughter, David. I don't need your two cents."

"I don't care. I'll gladly give it because she is my niece, and she deserves to be treated with respect. She is a sweet little girl and you're a *monster*," David scolded.

"Oh fuck off. You don't even know what it's like to have a daughter," Mother replied.

I gasped with everyone else in the room.

"Jesus, Violet! Why would you say that?" Vanya asked.

"That...that was a cruel thing to say to me, Violet." David stared down at the floor with glossy eyes.

"Are you gonna say anything or are you just gonna stand there?" Mother was pointing at Father as he shook his head.

"David is right. That was completely unnecessary. It's Christmas and we have guests who will probably never come to our house ever again. I wouldn't blame them. You have humiliated the both of us. You thought Vanya would embarrass us with her drinking? No one cares. You're the only one. You're always the one who gives a shit about the stupidest things ever," Father said calmly.

"Oh, of course. You always side with your little brother. You might as well make love to him and not me," Mother hissed.

"You're disgusting, Violet," David snapped.

She stomped away and went outside, steaming. Everyone stayed quiet for a while as I went back to Arthur and snuggled underneath his arm.

"I'm so sorry," I whispered.

"Don't be."

"I hope you still love me."

"Oh please. My brother Barry tackled my dad to the floor last Christmas because he thought he touched Caroline's ass. This is pretty tame."

"I guess we both won the family lottery." I dryly laughed.

"Merry Christmas, huh?"

"Merry Christmas, Arthur."

"Sorry about all the excitement everyone. Families argue, couples argue but at the end of the day we all love each other. It happens. Let's try to enjoy the rest of the night." Father broke the silence.

Arthur and I decided to stay put after that disaster. Vanya ended up going to Vera's room to comfort her while my Father and David cleaned up the mess my Mother had made. Next thing I knew I had fallen asleep. When I woke up, I heard my Father and David speaking in hushed tones while they had a drink. I pretended to stay asleep to eavesdrop.

"You should've never married that woman. She's an evil bitch," David hissed.

"She's my wife and she wasn't always that way."

"She treats your daughters like shit. I wanna fucking strangle her for what she did to Vera tonight."

"You're angry. You wouldn't hurt a fly."

"I'd kill for your daughter. I'd kill for Vera if I had to," David warned.

"You're a good brother, David. Let's go to the backyard. I don't wanna wake them." Father chuckled.

My Father thought he was joking but David sounded serious. He wasn't someone who joked around like Vanya. When they left, I decided to get up and go out for some fresh air. Arthur was dead asleep, so I let him be. When I went out, I saw Barry talking with the neighbor, Walter Campbell. I didn't hear much before they saw me, but I did overhear that Walter wanted to keep in touch. I always did find that a little strange. That was where Barry met Walter. It was on that Christmas Day. That was when their relationship started. That was where I wished I had heard what Barry and Walter had been talking about. I would've seen the warning signs a lot sooner.

CHAPTER 6
PRESENT DAY

I went to the St. Devil police station when I learned the name of the detective who handled David's case. A Detective Peter Jurgen. He was retired but I managed to get a phone number from one of the cops working the front desk. I called him and he agreed to meet me if I bought him a cup of coffee from *Devil's Brew*. An old-school coffee shop that was on its last legs. It had a creaky wooden front door with no handle, a burned-out neon sign and a vintage interior with cracked, checkered floors. We sat in a red leather booth as a waitress brought us two cups of piping hot, freshly brewed coffee.

Detective Jurgen was in his early 60s. He had wily grey hair, a pair of round glasses and was a stout, rectangular figure with a protruding beer belly. His bloodshot eyes popped when he loudly slurped his coffee. I could tell he had lived off caffeine his entire law enforcement career.

"I'm only speaking to you because you helped catch that bastard Kenneth Kilhouser."

"My source gave your department the anonymous tip first. It fell on deaf ears."

Detective Jurgen stretched back and clicked his tongue.

"Truth is, we had so many false tips we couldn't keep up. It's a good thing you were persistent and followed up on that tip. If you didn't, it would've fallen through the cracks," Detective Jurgen said.

"I know. I wasn't about to let that happen."

"What can I help you with?"

"You handled my uncle's suicide case. In your personal opinion, do you think David Snow could've hired someone to kill Violet Snow, my mother, and my Aunt Vanya Reyes?"

Detective Jurgen rubbed his chin in deep thought.

"No, I don't think so. He died years before any of them were killed. It wouldn't make sense."

"Well, I'm not saying he succeeded. I think something very bad may have happened. David might've changed his mind which led to some hired asshole possibly killing him and staging his suicide."

"Ah, you're referring to the wild theories that were circling my department at the time of that investigation. The biggest thing of course was that suspicious phone number he had on his suicide note. We found several past owners but none of them were sketchy enough to warrant a closer look. We later learned that your Father also contacted several individuals, but nothing came up. The trail ran cold. So we closed the case as a suicide." Detective Jurgen explained.

"Now that I think about it, how does he have that suicide note?"

"We gave him a copy."

"That's allowed?"

"He was knocking down our doors trying to find answers on what happened. He threatened to light our department on fire through the press. Your Father is a powerful man. We obliged because we didn't want any issues. He left us alone after that. Thank god."

It didn't surprise me. That's who my Father was. The man who busted down doors to get what he wanted.

"Do you think it was a suicide?"

"Well...no. No, Venus. I thought it was a...murder," Detective Jurgen said gravely.

"Why? What did you find?"

Detective Jurgen shuffled uncomfortably and glanced around, nervously.

"What's wrong?" I asked.

"A cold shiver runs down my spine whenever I think about David's case. I feel like someone is watching me. Someone who knows the truth. The way the rope was put around his neck was strange because of the angle and the position. The ligature marks around his neck are so deep it looks like someone was strangling him. He wouldn't have been able to do that to himself. David's neck was crushed, and all signs pointed to it being very rushed. It seemed like he was in danger, but we never found anything to suggest that someone was after him and your family said he was in good spirits. It just didn't make any sense. It looked like someone staged it." Detective Jurgen urged.

It felt like a bullet had ripped through my heart. I didn't know about any of that. It was the first time I had heard about it. All my life I was sure Uncle David had killed himself. That truth was shattered the moment Detective Jurgen believed that he had been *murdered*. That changed everything. The deaths of Violet, Vanya,

Vera, and David were all related one way or another. If they were all murdered...that meant that the serial killer was targeting my family.

"That's absolutely horrifying."

"I'm sorry. I won't give you any more gruesome details about your dead uncle. Why are you asking about him anyway? Does this have to do with..."

"The murders in my family? Yeah, it does. I think there's a serial killer after us and they won't stop until we're all dead."

"Have you spoken with the detective on Vanya and Vera's case?"

"Only twice. They haven't followed up. I don't know if they're gonna find something or if they're gonna find jack shit. I'm doing this on my own. I'm not gonna wait around until I get kidnapped and stabbed in a dark alley. I'm not gonna make it easy for them."

"Fair enough. I hope you're being very careful."

I was being as careful as possible, but you can only be so safe when you're tracking down an actual *serial killer*.

"Did the handwriting on the suicide note match David's?"

"It was heavily suspected that it was forged but we never went deeper into the case. Resources were limited."

What the hell went on in David's case?

"That's really great."

"Believe me, no one was as frustrated as I was on that case. I really hope you catch that piece of shit killing your family."

"I don't really have a choice. I have to, or I'll probably die."

"I think you're too stubborn to die." Detective Jurgen grinned while drinking the last of his coffee.

We'll see detective. We'll see if death comes for me.

Detective Jurgen suggested I visit David's old apartment building. I went to go see his old neighbor, Polly Westphal. It was a quiet building with a rickety elevator, peeling walls and a strong, metallic odor that was off-putting. The years had not been kind to it. Thankfully Polly still lived at apartment 207 and was kind enough to invite me in for tea.

She was an older woman with frazzled dark-grey hair that looked like she had been electrocuted. She wore a large fur coat and pristine, white slippers. She wore dentures and was a self-proclaimed mother to 7 cats. I remembered Uncle David saying she was extremely nice but clinically insane. She had a portrait above her old box TV set that was a detailed painting of herself along with an army of cats surrounding her as she laid half-naked on a cat-themed rug. I took David's word for it. I sat down on her plastic-covered couch and tried not to spit out the scalding hot cup of tea I had sipped.

"So, you're here to discuss poor David Snow?" Polly asked.

"I am. I was wondering if you had any information that could help in my investigation into his suicide."

"Oh my, I thought that case was closed. Did something new come up?"

"Not exactly, but...well my family has been...murdered." I swallowed.

"Oh my goodness. I always forget things. I'm so sorry dear. I heard about that. I've seen your face on the news. Everyone in St. Devil knows about you I think. Horrible, horrible business! Only people who believe in Satan do things like that." Polly's voice shook with anger.

I didn't want to get into my family's murders again, so I quickly redirected her.

"Polly, what did you think about David? Were you two friends or anything?" I asked.

"Oh heavens yes! He was very kind. Quiet, but kind. He wasn't the type of person to jump up and down in excitement, but he did always help me put away my groceries. A true gentleman," Polly said.

"Did you notice anything strange on the night he died?"

"Sweetie, I honestly can't remember. It was so long ago. However, you wanna know what I think? I think he saw something he shouldn't have and was killed for it. So many evil people in the world."

"You're not wrong."

"Or he could've been very depressed because of his wife's death. It might be possible he chose not to live anymore. She had a miscarriage you know. They were gonna have a daughter. David was really sad about that," Polly said.

"I considered that, but his wife had died so many years before. If he wanted to do it, I believe he would've done it back then. The miscarriage was also many years before her death. But...I don't know. Maybe he never truly got over it. How could he? He lost his family."

David had all the reasons in the world to end it all when he lost his baby and when his wife passed away due to a terrible, ravaging illness. He was trapped in a storm of unrelenting pain and grief when that happened. My Father helped him get through it and he became very close to Vera, loving her like his own daughter. My Father and Vera saved his life by pulling him out of the deep, dark muck he had sunk into. We thought he was doing much better as the years went on. Maybe we were wrong.

"Despite the things that happened to him, I'm not convinced David killed himself. I don't think he would've done that to his brother. Dennis did so much for him." Polly wiped her runny nose and scanned the room.

Definitely something off about her.

"Is there anything else you remember about that night?"

"Yes. I remember Dennis' screams when he found David's dead body hanging from the ceiling. It was very painful to hear. Dennis loved his brother very much. That much was clear."

If only he loved me and Vera that much.

"I have one last question. Is there anyone else who lived here during the time David lived here? Any neighbors from back then who are still around?"

"Lee Smith is one man who still lives on this floor. He's right next door to David's old apartment."

"I'll see if he's home."

"No, no, no! Don't bother speaking with him. He's very rude and mean. He won't pay you any mind." Polly waved her hand dismissively.

"Alright, well thank you for your time, Polly. I appreciate this." I got up and affectionately touched her arm.

"Oh, you're very welcome *Vena*."

There's no point in correcting her.

I noticed there were several grocery bags filled with food items in her kitchen. She noticed me looking at them and smiled, slowly nodding.

"You need help?"

"If you would be so kind!"

"Of course."

In a strange way, she reminded me of Aunt Vanya. The funny mannerisms and the very chic clothing was uncanny. She could've been an older Vanya without a doubt. I swiftly wiped my tears away before Polly could see.

When I said farewell to Polly and stepped outside, I saw an elderly Asian man fumbling his keys near his apartment door while he had a small bag of lemons in his other hand. He was angrily muttering to himself as he tried to find the right key. I decided to ignore Polly's advice and slowly approached him.

"Hi, are you Lee Smith?"

"What? Who are you?" Lee glanced at me with a scowl.

"My name is Venus Duarte. David Snow was my uncle. You were his neighbor."

"Listen, Venus, I don't want to talk about a man killing himself. It's very ugly business and I already answered all of Detective Jurgen's questions back then. I don't want to talk about that anymore. The case was closed," Lee said firmly.

My insides were boiling but I had to keep my cool. He was an older man. I didn't want to yell at him.

"That's okay, I understand. Do you need help with that?" I asked softly.

"No I don't need any help lady. I was in the war. I don't need to talk about death anymore. I can't even get my lemons in peace." Lee grumbled.

"Have a nice day," I said through gritted teeth.

I had to leave before I developed the urge to smash his lemons on the floor.

I loathed my Father's invitations. I usually refused to go or ignored them completely, but this time was different. It was a benefit at an art exhibition for Vanya and Vera. My Father was starting a new charity that was named after them. The proceeds would go to female victims of domestic violence and femicide. How generous of him. My Father was a living irony. His ego was so blinding he couldn't realize how strange it was that he didn't add Violet's name to the charity, even if it was his ex-wife. She had her head chopped off too. She deserved something.

I wore a sparkly black dress that accentuated my curves while Arthur wore a sleek, black tuxedo with a red rose pinned to his left breast. I heard my Mother's shrill voice as I put the dress on.

How can you show that much skin?

Why doesn't it go below your knees?

It looks very, very tight.

Your belly is showing. You shouldn't have eaten that double cheese-burger. So fattening.

Everyone is going to be staring and whispering. I hope you know that.

I silently screamed in my head so she would go away and tried to quiet my mind. I focused on the task at hand. I would go in and greet my Father. I would walk around for an hour while pretending to enjoy the bizarre, incomprehensible art pieces. I would then promptly leave before my Father would make me speak to his dumb rich buddies.

The exhibit was being held at a stylish art museum that was a white stone building with decorative columns at every corner. When we entered I saw that the space was carefully designed with soft lighting, subdued wall colors and an intricate layout that allowed for a seamless viewing experience. There was a various array of paintings, sculptures, photographs, and digital art pieces that all revolved around a single theme. *Your Inner Demon Can Be Conquered.* It was about the idea that most people live with an inner demon that is never conquered. This demon can rule and ruin your life. He wanted people to step back and reflect on ways the inner demon could be destroyed. It was a motivation thing for people in business or something. It was easier to reflect if you were filthy rich, but I got the idea. My Father wanted people to conquer their inner demons. *My own Father.* I wanted to tear everything down piece by piece. I felt personally insulted by that sneering bastard.

I was examining an ominous painting that had a white figure with bright red eyes running from a sprawling black cloud with sharp, thick tendrils. It seemed like it wanted to impale its target. There was a dark farmhouse in the background. While I tried to reflect, Arthur was staring into space, bored out of his mind.

"Are you going crazy?" I asked him, squeezing his shoulder.

"Me? Oh no. I'm good. This is a very cool event. I like all the art. It's artsy."

He'd never admit it. He was as steady as they came. He would always be there for me when I needed him and I for him.

"Don't worry, we'll be leaving soon."

"Okay. I'm gonna find a bathroom."

As soon as he left, I felt a tangible presence behind me, staring at me. When I glanced back, it was my Father. He was observing the painting with keen eyes.

"This is one of my favorite ones. I had it commissioned with my own vision. I liken it to the darkness within us all. We are all white figures, and we all try to escape the dark urges and impulses that can fester inside of us if we're not careful. It could become deadly and all-consuming."

"You relate to it very much. I'm not surprised."

"Are you going to hate me forever, Venus?" Father scoffed.

"I'd like to."

Father chortled like it was an actual joke. I glared at him and shook my head.

"You're a funny girl, Venus. Remember, I'm the only family you have left. We only have each other. Violet, Vanya, and Vera are all dead."

And I'm sure you had something to do with that.

I wanted to scream that at him. I wanted to shout it from the rooftops, but I couldn't. Not yet anyway. I needed evidence. I had to continue with the investigation. I had to leave no doubt. I had to cross all the suspects off my list until he was the only one remaining. If he ended up being the only one left anyway.

"I know that. You don't have to remind me."

"Detective Jurgen gave me a call. He told me you were asking around about David."

"That was fast."

"We have a good relationship. I'm friends with many cops."

I don't think friends is the right word.

"That's convenient," I remarked.

"Why are you going around, asking questions?"

"I report true crime. You know this," I said, the irritation noticeable in my voice.

"I do. You're trying to find a serial killer. That's very dangerous work, Venus."

"I am shocked that you know that."

"I keep up with what my daughter is doing."

"I guess it's easy because you only have one now."

Father coldly stared at me, and I was forced to meet his eyes.

"Why do you say horrible things like that?"

"I...I don't know."

I did know, but I didn't want to say it then. He'd never get it. He never thought he did anything wrong to me when I was a child. He never apologized and he barely acknowledged it. He usually just laughed it off or justified it as silly little punishments he doled out to keep me in line. They weren't silly little punishments. He left me with bruises, black eyes, and fractured bones. My left index finger was still deformed from when he snapped it in half. He refused to get me medical help that day and when my Mother eventually found out, she almost broke his head with a lamp.

Just one of many incidents that shaped the dark terror that was my childhood.

"Are you talking to anyone else?"

"I don't think that's any of your business, dad."

"I'm your Father. It is my business. I need you to stay safe. I don't know what I would do if you died too."

"I'm not gonna die. I'm trying to find the serial killer that's decimating our family. You can stay out of it. I'm handling it," I snapped.

"Are you sure you want to get in the crosshairs of that sadistic bastard?"

"I helped catch Kenneth Kilhouser. He was a serial killer. I'll be just fine."

"You got lucky."

"Thank you for believing in me, like always." I stomped away before he could say anything else.

I wasn't interested in what other garbage he wanted to spew. He had no idea what he actually was. He had been lying to himself for so long that he started believing that what he had done was somehow morally correct.

As I went to look for Arthur, David's puzzling case came to mind. There was a strong chance that he had been murdered, but his head was never chopped off. Why was he killed? Why would they stage his suicide? What the hell happened that night? The trail had run cold for the time being, but I knew that if I continued on, I would find the answers I was looking for. It was all connected in some way. It was time to visit my parents' old neighbor.

CHAPTER 7

There was still a huge question on nearly everyone's mind in St. Devil. Why did Walter Campbell go missing? Why did he disappear without a trace? Why did he seemingly vanish at almost the exact same time my mother was murdered? To that day he still hadn't been found. It was the most bizarre missing persons case in St. Devil's history.

I visited his wife Sandra at her home. She was gracious enough to let me in. It felt like a haunted house when I entered. There were framed vacation pictures of Walter and Sandra on almost every wall and furniture stand in the living room. The shades were drawn which made the house dark. Sandra looked like she hadn't seen the sunlight in years. She was a short, very pale woman with a dark brown bob cut. Sandra's brown eyes had dark circles around them which told me everything I needed to know. That poor woman was suffering because of her husband's disappearance. I didn't blame her one bit. How could you live knowing that you had no idea where your husband was and why he disappeared? I thought about Arthur. The idea was enough to make me go into a full-blown panic.

We sat down across from each other at a small wooden table. As I prepared my notes, she stared at the table, unflinching. It was like a big part of her had died. It seemed like she was hanging on one thread. The possibility that Walter was still alive. At that point I wasn't so sure that was possible.

"Thank you so much for taking the time to talk with me, Sandra. I know this is very hard for you."

"Only you would understand, Venus. I'm so sorry for everything that's happened to you. We haven't had easy lives as of late," Sandra said quietly.

"Well, that's why I'm doing this. I'm trying to figure out who murdered my family and in doing so, I hope to find answers regarding Walter's disappearance."

"I miss him so much," Sandra sobbed.

I reached over and touched her hand.

"I know," I whispered.

I didn't know the best thing to do in those situations. So I did what I used to do with my sister. I would hold her hand, squeeze her shoulder or embrace her while I repeated to her that everything was going to be okay. That was the only thing I could say and the only thing we could hope for. Unfortunately in our case, life never became okay until many years later. Even that period was short-lived.

"I'm sorry, I'm sorry. I get emotional whenever I think about my Walter." Sandra wiped her eyes, and I offered her some tissues.

"I've read up on Walter's case and I know that he went missing the night of Caroline Duarte's funeral. Which was also the same night my mom was murdered. He met up with some friends at a bar after the service and was supposed to go home but he never made it."

"That is correct. He sent me a text message telling me that he was going home but he never came. I assumed he fell asleep at some friend's house because he was drunk. When he didn't come home the next day, I knew something was wrong. I tried calling him and texting, but he never ever answered. So I reported it to the police," Sandra explained.

"It seems his phone was turned off or destroyed because it stopped sending pings at around 3:32 AM. This was the morning after he went to the bar."

"Walter's phone was always on. He always answered my calls and messages, so I know something bad happened to him. One can only pray and hope he's still alive."

"You don't have any children correct?"

"We don't. We chose not to have any. As a result we became everything to each other. Without him, I don't feel complete. I don't even feel like I'm a real person anymore."

"I know how that feels."

"The fact that his car is missing too, and that it's never been found leads me to believe that someone might've abducted him. Why would someone want to hurt him? I'm not sure."

"What type of car did he have again?"

"It's a 1972 Firebird."

I took a mental note of that.

"Is there anything at all that would lead you to believe that he was doing something he wasn't supposed to? Maybe he got himself into some trouble. He could've been involved with the wrong people."

In my experience, people didn't just disappear like that. They typically had skeletons in their closet. The fact that Walter went missing at nearly the same time my mother was murdered raised alarm bells in my head. Was Walter the killer? Or was he another victim?

Sandra slowly lifted her head and looked me in the eyes for the first time since I started talking to her. She folded her hands together and pursed her lips. She opened her mouth hesitantly and her breathing was shallow. I wasn't sure if she was experiencing a sudden medical emergency or if she was about to tell me to fuck off.

"I loved Walter with all my heart, but I had my suspicions," Sandra sighed.

"What suspicions?"

"I thought he was cheating on me."

My heart skipped a beat. That was new. I had never thought of the possibility of Walter cheating on his wife. I quickly wondered if that had something to do with his disappearance. Did he escape with some secret lover somewhere?

"What led you to believe that?" I asked.

"He started carrying a lot of cash with him all of a sudden. At first I thought he was selling drugs but that was a ridiculous idea. I thought he was bored with his life and wanted to try something exciting. It turns out he was bored but he wasn't taking drugs. He got the excitement he wanted in another way. *Open Legs.*" Sandra raised her eyebrows.

"What?"

"It's a strip club near the edge of town. I found a business card in his jacket pocket from a presumed dancer named Diamond. I confronted him about it. He became very defensive and told me it was a silly prank one of his friends had played on him. He would never go to a strip club in a million years, he said. I called the number on the card, but it was out of service. I didn't bother to do anything further," Sandra explained.

"Did you really think it was just a prank?"

"No, I never did. He became careless with his lies, and I caught him red-handed. He had a lot of cash in his pockets, he was coming home late, and he smelled like cigarette smoke. He had never smoked a day in his life. Things weren't adding up. We weren't having sex that often either. I put two and two together."

"Do you still have the business card?"

"I do." Sandra got up and went to the living room.

I couldn't believe it. Walter Campbell was an alleged adulterer. The man who had baked apple pies for my sister and I when we were little was getting lap dances from strippers who had business cards. Another man with a mask and a lot of secrets.

"Here you are."

Sandra returned and handed me the card. It was a wrinkled, black card with the name *DIAMOND – EXOTIC DANCING SER-VICES* emblazoned on the front. On the back was a phone number, **505-555-0005**. As Sandra sat down, I almost fell out of my chair. I tightly gripped it and examined it very closely. I realized it was the same number that was scrawled on David's suicide note. Why the hell did David have the phone number of a stripper on his suicide note?

"I gave it to the detective, but they never followed up with me. I had no idea what to do next. I've been waiting for answers ever since."

"Thank you so much, Sandra. I'm going to look into this."

I shook her hand and exited her house as fast as possible. I needed to go to *Open Legs* and find Diamond. As I unlocked my car door, I felt someone watching me. I peered across the street and saw a dark figure staring at me. The streetlight above him was out so I only saw a tall, dark shape. I instinctively rubbed my belly as a suffocating knot formed in my stomach. I decided to ignore it and went inside. When I started to back out, I quickly looked in the rearview mirror. The dark figure was suddenly gone. I rubbed my eyes and questioned on whether or not I had actually seen it. My mind liked to play tricks on me. I thought I was going nuts.

A burgeoning ball of anxiety festered in my stomach and threatened to cripple my bodily functions. I had to slowly breathe in and out to calm down. I wouldn't crash the car in a frenzied panic. I refused to. An ear-splitting phone ring made me jump and woke me right up. I frantically answered it to stop the booming sound. It was Arthur. I wished I hadn't answered it. I already knew what was in store.

"Hey baby, where are you?"

"I'm driving to a strip club."

"You're going where?"

"It's related to my investigation."

"*Oh, okay. When will you be home?*"

"*I can't be sure, but hopefully soon.*"

"*It's getting really late.*"

"*I know Arthur.*"

"*Alrighty, be careful please. I'll see you later. Love you.*"

"*Love you too.*" I hung up and sighed. I hated talking to him in a rushed, annoyed tone but I was on the cusp of discovering something important in my investigation. Deep down, I knew he didn't take it that seriously. He would much rather have me home to be *safe*. He thought I was on a crazy vendetta that would lead to nowhere. He was wrong.

Open Legs was situated in a dingy parking lot on the less favorable side of town. The entrance had an unassuming façade that gave way to a dimly lit interior. A bouncer stood guard. He was checking IDs and making sure all the men paid the fee upfront. I was ushered in with no issues on my end.

"Free drinks for you, sweetheart," the bouncer commented. I nodded and smiled, ready to play the part.

Once inside, I stepped into a pulsating, sensual world of flashing lights, rhythmic music, and sultry strippers. They were twerking their hearts away to a sea of old, disgusting men who shouted horrible things and threw bills at them. I made my way to the bar and didn't even have to ask for anything. A drink was promptly given to me by the bartender who told me to enjoy the night. I held up my finger and told him to come closer. He was on the younger side and had a faded haircut along with black barbell earrings and a thin mustache.

"Hey, I need some information," I shouted over the music.

"What kind of information, baby?" He asked coyly.

"I'm married, kid."

"That's interesting. What are you doing in a strip club? Sounds like your husband isn't giving you what you want."

"What the hell are you talking about?" My anger was rising through my gut like a volcano preparing to explode.

"I know how to satisfy a beautiful woman. I'm free after work tonight." He winked.

I looked around the club. I saw that it was dark enough for me to aggressively grab ahold of his collar and pull him closer.

"I'm not here to fuck around. Is there a stripper named Diamond who works here?" The bartender's eyes bulged, and he held up his hands in surrender.

"Yes, she's here tonight. If she's not on the floor, she'll be in the dressing room. Please don't hurt me." He squeaked.

"What does she look like?"

"She has long black hair, dark skin and wears heavy makeup. She has really thick thighs too."

"Thank you, have a good night." I let go of him in disgust and glared at him as I slid away into the dancing crowd. He nervously fixed his collar and rubbed his watery eyes.

I'm not your baby. Punk-ass kid. I thought.

I was relieved no one had seen that because I couldn't stand other people looking at me when I was mad like that. I didn't like losing control. It made me feel a sharp pain in the pit of my stomach that warned my body that I needed to calm down before things got out of hand.

I scanned all the stripping poles and shoved away drunk men as I searched for Diamond. I didn't see her, so I looked for the dressing room. There was an opening in the wall at the end of the club with an entrance that had drapes. Above it, it said *DANCERS ONLY.* There were two buff security guards standing watch so I couldn't just waltz in. I saw two very intoxicated old men and formulated a plan. I strutted over to them and caught their attention.

"Oh wow hello." One of them said.

"You're so beautiful and sexy...beautiful. I want to kiss you with tongue." The other one said. He had rotting teeth and made me want to gag.

"Look, I overheard that stripper over there wanted a couple of guys to rush the stage to dance with her." I took out two $50 bills and handed one to each of the drunkards.

"Are you serious? She wants us?"

"Sure."

I watched in amusement as they rushed the stage and started awkwardly dancing with one of the strippers. The stripper screamed for security, and I felt a pang of guilt, but I knew she would be fine. I needed to get to Diamond. As I snuck over to the dancers' dressing room, the two buff security guards raced towards the commotion as the two drunkards were tackled to the ground. I managed to discreetly enter my destination amidst the chaos on the dance floor.

I took a short hallway towards a big room with a massive, rectangular mirror and barstool-like chairs scattered all around the linoleum floor. There were silver racks with sets of lingerie, fishnets, scarfs, animal-print jackets, and leggings. A shoe rack held a large row of pole shoes. I spotted a woman near them, trying shoes on. She matched the description that the horny bartender had given me. I slowly approached her.

"Hi. Are you Diamond?"

She flinched and quickly turned around, shoe in hand. She pointed it at me like a gun and scowled at me.

"Who the hell are you? How'd you get in here? Security!" She shouted.

"No, no, no, wait. Please. My name is Venus Duarte. All I want is some information and I'll be on my way."

"What kind of information?"

"Are you Diamond?"

"It depends."

"Do you know Walter Campbell?"

"I have no idea who that is."

"Really? Because your business card was in his jacket pocket."

"That doesn't mean shit. Get the hell out of here."

"Please, I'm not with the police. I'm trying to figure out why he went missing."

"Why?"

"I think he might be a serial killer."

Diamond tossed the shoe aside and sat down.

"You have my attention. Yes, I'm Diamond. Why the hell do you think Walter is a serial killer? That is some crazy shit."

"He went missing around the same time my mother Violet, was murdered. My Aunt Vanya and my little sister Vera were also murdered in the same way, months later. They were butchered by some kind of axe and their heads were sliced off. I'm the only remaining woman in my family."

Diamond held her trembling hand up to her mouth.

"Holy shit, you're that girl. You're that true crime social media chick. You helped catch that guy...Kilhouser. Your family...your family was killed."

"Yeah." I whispered.

"I'm so sorry, girl. That is some evil shit. Whoever did that needs to be ripped apart by the devil himself."

"Whoever did this...is the devil himself."

Diamond stayed silent and slowly nodded in agreement.

"I know what it's like to lose someone like that. I lost my mom to domestic violence. My daddy beat her head against a wall until chunks of her brain became a part of the paint. His jealously killed her."

I shuddered. That was not a pretty sight to imagine, but one that was all too real.

"I'm sorry that happened to you."

"Me too. Listen, I knew Walter Campbell. He was a regular here and he always gave out the fattest cash tips. He was convinced he was in love with me. He wasn't the first. When he went missing, the police came around here and started asking questions. No one said anything. We don't talk to the police. We don't trust them."

"Do you trust me?"

Diamond eyed me up and down. She grinned.

"You seem alright. I know you from the true crime shit so that gives you points. I also figure that you probably live in a nice white neighborhood where immigrants cut your lawn."

"You hit it on the nose."

"That's okay. It's not your fault. We were born on opposite sides of St. Devil."

And yet here we both are...experiencing the same gruesome violence at the hands of monsters wearing human skin.

"If you know Walter Campbell, did you know a David Snow by chance? He was my uncle."

"Name doesn't ring a bell." Diamond clucked her tongue.

I slid my phone out of my pocket and scrolled for a picture of him. I held it up and walked closer to her. She bent forward and squinted her eyes, examining it.

"I've never seen that guy in my life," Diamond said, shaking her head.

"It's strange. Your phone number was on his suicide note."

"Well, shit. That's messed up."

"Why do you think your number was there?"

"My *old* number. I don't use that anymore. Venus, I'll be honest I don't know. That's weird as hell. The only thing I can think of is…maybe Walter gave it to David. Was David lonely or something?" Diamond asked.

"David's wife was dead at the time of his suicide. I guess he was pretty lonely."

"Maybe Walter wrote it down for him once and when David went to off himself, he used that paper for convenience or something. Maybe he just didn't care anymore. Maybe he felt so guilty that he was about to call up a stripper that he wanted people to know that after he died."

"That's plausible."

"People do crazy shit that may not make sense at the time. It only makes sense when you start to really think about it. You have to think about their state of mind."

A stripper with philosophical musings? I have seen it all.

"I'll keep that in mind."

"You wanna know anything else? I gotta get on stage soon. A girl has to make a living."

"Did Walter ever tell you anything about moving away or escaping his life? It's clear to me now that he was unhappy, but how far do you think he would go to disappear forever?" I asked.

"I'm not really sure, to be honest. But I will tell you one thing, he was a huge mess. He started doing coke shortly after he started coming here and I quickly learned that Walter loved to spill the beans when he was drunk. He admitted to me that he was buying cocaine from a city official in a *snazzy uniform*. He also told me he was stepping out with a lovely lady outside of the club."

Sandra was wrong. Walter was using drugs after all.

"Did he ever say her name?"

"I don't remember. I know she was some rich chick who had money because her husband was some big shot who had properties. I think they were neighbors," Diamond said.

Neighbors? No. It can't be. It doesn't make any sense.

"Are you absolutely sure?"

"Oh, I'm positive. He talked about it all the time. It was a cool last name—, Snow! He said he used to step out with a lady named Miss Snow. She was married and she was his neighbor."

"Miss Snow."

"Yep."

Miss Snow was my mother. Violet Snow.

CHAPTER 8
12 YEARS EARLIER

By the time I was 21 years old I thought my home life would be better. It wasn't. It was still as chaotic, violent, and unforgiving as ever. I was foolish for hoping that things would improve while my Father was around. As long as he still breathed and treaded through the halls of our house, we were all stuck under his umbrella of hell.

When Vera was younger, she liked to play with the dolls in her dollhouse. She always asked me to join, and I could never say no to her adorable little face. All I needed to see was her radiant smile when I agreed to play, and my heart would immediately melt with joy. She was a beacon of innocence and love. I needed that. Without her, I never would've survived. The darkness that was my life would've overtaken me eventually.

In the dollhouse was a mother with three children. We were role-playing. The story was that the three children had suddenly disappeared one night, and we had to figure out why.

"Maybe they all went out for ice cream and forgot to go back home," Vera said.

"Maybe they all fell into a hole in the ground."

"Maybe they took a ride on a magical unicorn, and they'll be back soon."

"Maybe they all got hit by a car."

"Oh my god no. You are crazy."

"Not as crazy as a unicorn. They don't exist."

"Yes they do. We just haven't seen them yet." Vera smiled.

"You're right. They're out there somewhere." I tucked Vera's flowery hair behind her ears.

"Maybe the three daughters are busy getting their mom a birthday gift and that's why they're missing! They wanna surprise her!" Vera beamed.

"Aww, that's sweet of them."

"Can that be the end of the story? Please?" Vera clasped her hands together and pouted.

I wanted the ending to be that the three daughters were missing because they were dead and buried in the house's backyard. The big reveal would've been that the mother was a crazed serial killer. I began having a strong interest in true crime from a young age, so I had a pretty active yet twisted imagination. I didn't want to scar Vera for life, so I encouraged her child-like wonders.

"Yes, it can be the end of the story."

"Yay!" Vera threw her arms around me and hugged me tightly. I hugged her back and caressed her soft curls.

"I love that ending." Vera whispered.

"Me too."

"I don't like mean things."

"Me neither, Vera."

"Promise me you'll never be mean."

I stopped caressing her and softly held a few locks of her hair in my hand. I almost broke out crying, but I held myself together. I loved Vera with all my heart. She represented everything I found pure and innocent in the world. I knew what love truly was when Vera was born. Whenever she was in danger or got hurt, I felt my heart threatening to burst wide open. That was love.

When my Father stormed into the house, all hell broke loose. He had a pained, infuriated look on his face and it was terrifying. I embraced Vera tightly and mentally prepared myself for what was to come. He immediately stepped forward and swiped at a vase, grabbing it, and smashing it to the ground. Vera shrieked and I rubbed her back, trying to keep her calm. My mother immediately came out of the kitchen and approached my Father. She looked at him and at the broken vase on the floor. She threw her hands up.

"Dennis, what's wrong?"

"He's dead. David's dead! *He's fucking dead*!" My Father brushed past my mother as he continued like a charging tornado. He began shoving couches, flipping tables, and punching holes in the wall while my poor mother tried to stop him.

"Dennis, please! Stop it! You're destroying the house!" My mother urged.

"Did you not fucking hear me, Violet?! David's dead! He hung himself! He put a rope around his neck and killed himself!" Father shouted so loudly the ground shook.

Vera was so terrified of our Father's anger she dug her face into my shoulder and sobbed. I felt the wet tears pouring out of her eyes and into my clothes. A twisting knot of anxiety formed in my stomach. It continued to expand as I saw my Father's face twist with increasing rage, second by second. He yanked a family portrait off the wall and raised it high in the air. He was prepared to catapult it into the floor.

"No Dennis! No! Stop it!" My mother grasped his arm and tried to get him to stop. He shrugged her off and smashed the portrait on her head, causing her to yell out in pain as she collapsed. The portrait was in half as my mother held up a hand in defense.

"Please Dennis. You hurt me. You hurt me really bad." My mother cried.

"You're so fucking annoying. My brother just died. You couldn't just leave me be?!" Father growled.

"Dad stop! Please! You're destroying everything!" I urged. I didn't know where I got the courage to even say that to my Father, but I did. I guess I was just so sick and tired of taking it from him. I wanted it to end already.

"You shut the hell up! You have no idea what I'm going through! You can fuck off!" Father commanded.

My mother slowly rose with her hand on her head. She quickly walked towards my sister and me. She gently pushed us to go upstairs.

"Go. Stay in your room until it's over." My mother whispered.

"Are you okay? Are you bleeding?"

"I'm fine. It's just a bump. Go. Do as I say."

"Mom, are you sure? Can I help?" I pleaded.

"No, not right now. You need to get out of here."

I guided Vera upstairs and into my bedroom as she continued to cry.

"We're gonna die, Venus. He's gonna kill us. Dad is gonna kill us." Vera choked out. She was sobbing so hard, she could barely control her breathing.

"No, that's not happening. Everything is going to be fine. I promise you." I softly massaged her head as I continued to hear screams coming from downstairs.

Please just talk to me! What happened to David?!

I already told you! He's dead!

Where are you going?! Put that baseball bat down, Dennis!

Leave me the hell alone!

I heard a whirlwind of crashes, thuds and shrieking as I closed my eyes and waited for it to be over. I covered Vera's ears so she wouldn't have to hear our Father calling our mother the most terrible things I had ever heard him say. Throughout the entire traumatic ordeal, I hadn't even processed what my Father was upset about.

Oh my god. Uncle David is...dead?

I hadn't seen any news or anything on the internet about his death, but it was crystal clear that he had died. My Father wouldn't have acted like that otherwise. Well, he would've, but this was more extreme. When I heard the front door being slammed shut I breathed out a sigh of relief. My stomach stopped erupting with pain and I felt somewhat calm again. My Father was gone. He had left. Where? Who the hell knew. I was just happy we didn't have to tolerate his wrath anymore. Something that unfortunately had become too common-place in my family and in my house.

PRESENT DAY

While I drove to Sandra Campbell's house, I strongly considered the possibility that my mother had cheated on my Father with Walter. What did that mean for her death? I wasn't quite sure yet. I needed more answers.

After David's death, my Father relentlessly accused my mother of cheating on him for a long time. After he saw her "flirting" with another man at the grocery store, something switched in his mind. A trigger was pulled, and my Father never let it go.

My mother would argue that she couldn't possibly be cheating because she was taking care of Vera at home most of the time. That was a bold-faced lie. I was the one who took care of Vera at home. My mother would usually be drugged up on pills, asleep or both. There were a few instances where I drove Vera to a friend's house for a party and when I came back home, my mother was gone. I always wondered why but never thought she'd be capable of such a thing. I thought my Father would be the one to cheat. It would've been easier for him.

I guess that since my Father was out of town so often for business, it finally got to her. She got sick of being alone and wanted to be satisfied romantically. It made me want to vomit all over myself. The thought of my mother being with another old man in a hotel room. It made my skin crawl and disgusted me very much.

I didn't agree with my mother's alleged actions, but I understood why she did it. When my Father would come back from a business trip, he would make no effort to make my mother feel special. It was like they weren't even married. He wouldn't plan anything, suggest anything, or show her any affection. That most likely made her feel like she was nothing. My Father was very good at making people feel like they were garbage.

When I got to the Campbell residence and parked I saw Sandra outside, staring at me. She was darting her eyes in multiple directions and seemed nervous. She was halfway inside her house while she tightly held the door, prepared to close it at a moment's notice. That wasn't a good sign. I sighed and steadily approached. She wagged her finger at me and shook her head.

"Hey Sandra."

"I changed my mind. This isn't a good idea. We can't speak."

"What's wrong?"

Sandra refused to look me in the eye as she peered over my shoulder and drummed her fingers on the side of her front door.

"There was a man. A very aggressive man."

A shiver went down my spine.

An aggressive man?

"He threatened me and told me not to speak to anyone regarding Walter's disappearance because it was still an ongoing investigation."

"Wait, how would he know that? Who was he?"

"It was a police officer. I didn't catch his name."

"What did he look like?"

Sandra hesitated and shook her head.

"I really shouldn't be telling you any of this. Listen, it's dark out and I need to go back inside."

"Please Sandra. I'm just trying to find answers. Who was this cop?"

"He has a lot of tattoos, and he's white. He has a slight accent. I think he's Latino. He...he has a buzzcut. He seems like a military type."

I thought about it for a few seconds then quickly realized that it was Barry, Arthur's brother.

"Was the cop's name Barry?" I asked.

"I don't know. I told you; I didn't catch his name."

"Did he properly address you when he visited you?"

"Umm...I guess. I don't know."

"Did he tell you that his name was Officer Duarte?"

A light bulb seemed to go off in Sandra's head as she slowly nodded.

"Oh, yes. That sounds very familiar."

"Thank you for your time, Sandra. I'm sorry to bother you. Have a good night."

As I walked back to my car I wondered why Barry would want Sandra to stay quiet. There was also only one way he knew I had been talking to her. He was the one who had been watching me. He was the dark figure that was stalking me the night I visited her. I knew that Barry and Walter had met at my family's Christmas party all those years ago. I figured that they did keep in touch after all. I wondered why. They seemed so different from each other. Were they just friends or was there something else going on? A lot of strange, sinister overtones followed Barry and Walter. It was hard to give them the benefit of the doubt. This was especially true in Barry's case. He had a troublesome past. I hadn't forgotten the hushed allegations that he had been the one to murder his own wife, Caroline.

As I drove back home, rain began to fall in a gentle drizzle. When I turned on my wipers I glanced at my rearview mirror and saw that there was a black pick-up truck trailing behind me. I almost missed it. I was on a seldom-used one-way road. I thought I had been alone. The truck didn't have its headlights on despite how dark it was. My heart began to race as I sped up a bit. The truck sped up as well.

"What the fuck is this?" I asked aloud.

I kept driving and got to a traffic light that was red. The truck behind me finally turned on their headlights and blinded me in the process. I didn't notice that someone had exited the truck until it was too late. I saw them for a split second as they pointed a gun straight at my car.

"Oh fuck!"

I ducked as several bullets clanged into my car, piercing the exterior. It sounded like thunder was crackling in the sky as the gunfire sliced through the silence of the night. I floored it and my car screeched forward. I narrowly avoided a turning car that was furiously beeping their horn at me. I gladly took it. If I had stayed at that red light I would've been a dead woman. As my car roared forward, my heart pounded in my ribcage. Sheer adrenaline was surging through my veins as I tightly gripped the steering wheel. I tried to make sense of what happened, but I was at a loss for words. My head was throbbing, and my thoughts were scrambled. All my body knew was that I needed to survive that night.

When I got home, the adrenaline kept me going. I jumped out of my car and checked the damage. There were a few bullet holes in the back but nothing vital seemed to be hit. I breathed a sigh of relief. I was alive. I couldn't believe that someone had tried to...*kill* me.

I decided to wait to tell Arthur what happened. I hoped he wouldn't notice the damage. It was a very delicate situation. How would I explain to my husband that I strongly believed...his own brother had attempted to shoot me and kill me?

CHAPTER 9

I was in bed with Arthur, unable to sleep. I kept thinking about the shooting. I was very close to meeting my dead family wherever they were. I had my nightstand lamp on while he furiously typed away on his work laptop. He had kept his word and was using protection during sex. Little did he know that his seed had already been planted. I thought about the pregnancy, and I considered telling him almost every day. He was my husband after all. But I knew I couldn't say a word. He'd freak out on me. Things were complicated enough. I chose to live with my secret, and I would accept the consequences after everything was said and done.

At the very least I decided to see an OB/GYN at my own risk to check up on things and to make sure our baby was okay. The whole shooting situation had thoroughly frightened me. It validated the threat to my life I knew I had. Thankfully, everything was fine. When she asked me about the father, I made up an excuse to leave. I saw a few nurses staring at me, but I hid my face long enough to get the hell out of there. I wasn't entertaining anyone's invasive questions.

Despite the scare I experienced, I needed to continue on. I needed to find the serial killer who slaughtered my family. Nothing else mattered to me until that was done. Perhaps that made me a heartless monster considering I had a baby growing inside of me but so be it. I didn't want my baby to grow up in the same terrifying situation I had grown up in.

I didn't want him or her to sense fear and terror in their hearts nearly every single day in their own house because of my fucked-up family history. Arthur was not my Father by any means, but it was a different kind of terror. One that involved all of my loved ones dead and gone with their heads sliced off their bodies. How could I explain that to my own child? At the very least I needed to reassure them that the killer was either dead or rotting in a prison cell.

I rubbed my belly, lost in thought. I dreamt of a future where I could be a mother and enjoy parenthood with Arthur. I realized that my heart wasn't completely frosted over with ice. There was a warm, soft spot that was solely reserved for an eventual baby that would make me believe that the world could be a better place after all.

A singular, beautiful purpose that I had secretly wanted so badly for so long. I had never admitted it to myself because I was terrified of more loss. I wouldn't be able to live anymore if my baby didn't make it. Destructive, negative thoughts clouded my head like a thunderstorm. Miscarriage, stillborn...or worse. I couldn't handle another loved one dying inside of me. It would eviscerate me. I wouldn't know how to go on. The grief would choke my heart until it stopped beating and I would fade into nothingness. It would definitively be the end of me.

I thought about the potential connection between Walter and Barry for hours on end until it hit me. Diamond had told me that Walter mentioned procuring cocaine from a city official in a *snazzy uniform*. A cop could be considered a city official, and he obviously wore a uniform. That could mean that Barry was selling Walter cocaine. That could've been the reason why they decided to stay in touch. It could also explain why Barry was threatening Sandra not to talk about Walter's disappearance. Could Barry be the reason he went missing? Was my mother somehow involved? Did she see something she shouldn't have? What if my mother's murder and Walter's disappearance were both caused by the same person? Did Barry kill them both? I trembled just thinking about it. I was going further down the rabbit hole.

Barry, Barry, Barry.

He does have his mental issues.

He is suspected of murdering his own wife.

Why isn't anyone looking at him more closely?

He's a cop and a war veteran, Venus. Let's be real here.

I turned towards Arthur and softly squeezed his elbow. He didn't move and only grunted as he was very focused on his work.

"Hey, I have to ask you something important."

"What's up, baby?"

"Does Barry sell drugs?"

Arthur came to an immediate halt and stopped typing. He looked up and turned to me, perplexed.

"I'm sorry, what?"

"I think I might be onto something. It hinges on whether or not Barry sells drugs," I said.

Arthur slowly closed his laptop and folded his arms. He stared at the ceiling for a minute before answering.

"I don't know if he does now, but in the past…he sold weed to guys in high school and he gave weed to girls who had sex with him. That's all I know."

My eyes widened and I slapped his arm.

"What the hell? Are you serious? You never told me this."

"It's not something I wanted to share about my brother. I'm ashamed enough. I'm related to him."

Arthur rarely got along with his brother. They both came from a broken family. Arthur chose to be different while Barry carried on the family tradition.

"You still could've told me."

"I don't trust him and I'm afraid of what he's capable of. He's a police officer with a gun. I'm sorry but I don't like to think about him. He's not stable."

"I don't like to think about him either, but here we are. He might be involved in all this, and I need to find out why."

"Venus, what did you find?"

"I think my mom cheated on my dad with her former neighbor Walter Campbell."

Arthur turned to me and gaped.

"What? No way."

"A stripper named Diamond told me that Walter was stepping out with a *Miss Snow*. I don't think it's totally out of the question. It would give my dad a reason to kill my mom and a reason for Walter to disappear forever. This is assuming my dad found out."

"That could mean Walter is actually...dead."

"Or he could be in hiding. Who knows."

"Wait a second. Why were you talking to a stripper named Diamond?"

"I talked to Walter's wife, Sandra. She led me to *Open Legs*. A strip club that Walter used to frequent."

"He used to go to a strip club? What the hell? Looks like Walter isn't the good neighbor after all. What does this have to do with Barry selling drugs though?"

"Diamond also told me that Walter said he was buying cocaine from a city official in a *snazzy uniform*. I think that city official could be a cop which would be Barry."

"This is strange, Venus. I don't know about all of this. It sounds like a conspiracy. Why do you think it's Barry?"

"I never told you this but...I think he's stalking me. I saw a dark figure the night I talked to Sandra. It looked like a guy, and he was staring at me. It was really fucking creepy. When I went back to follow up with her, she told me a white cop with a buzzcut, and heavy tattoos threatened her to stay quiet. He had a slight accent and he seemed military like," I said.

"Shit. That does sounds like him."

"She told me the name *Officer Duarte* sounded really familiar."

Arthur rubbed his eyes and sunk below the covers.

"Let me get this straight. You think Barry is trying to silence Sandra because Walter's disappearance is connected to him."

"I'm positive that it is."

"You're saying that it's possible that my own brother killed Walter."

"I'm sorry, Arthur. I know that's not something you wanna hear. No one wants to hear that type of shit."

"He's my brother but he's a real piece of work. I guess that something like this was bound to come up sooner or later. The chickens are coming home to roost." Arthur sighed.

"He could also know if my mom really did cheat on Walter. I'm sure it came up."

"Even if he doesn't know that he must know something else. He has to have some information on *something*."

"Will you help me?"

"What do you need me to do?"

"I need you to find out what your brother has done."

"Okay." Arthur breathed in deeply and took my hand.

"Thank you," I said with a soft voice.

"Anything to help you get past this."

"I'll pay him a visit first."

"What? Why? Hell no. You're not gonna be alone with him in that house."

"I'm not going inside."

"That still worries me."

"What was the last thing you told him?"

"I...I told him to fuck off forever."

"Exactly."

"This isn't a good idea."

"He's not gonna do anything to me. He's smarter than that."

"My brother isn't smart, Venus."

I ruffled his hair. I needed him to let me see him. I wanted to look him in the eye and see the darkness I needed to see. I needed to know if there was real cause for Arthur to risk his life. Barry was a big talker when he was drunk, and I wasn't sure where that would lead to. Walter had that in common with him.

"I won't be there long. I promise. I'm gonna go there on your behalf and tell him that you want to see him. You can't just show up. This needs to look normal. Remember, he was watching me. He must know what's going on."

He was also probably shooting at me, but we don't need to talk about that yet.

"If he knows what's going on why would he tell me anything in the first place?"

"He probably won't, but you need to stay there late, and you need him to fall asleep. That's when you'll check his house for clues."

"You think he left anything there?"

"He's a cop who got away with murder. He thinks he's invincible."

"*Alleged murder.*"

I squinted my eyes at him.

"Let's be real. Who else would have done it?"

Arthur softly shook his head. He knew that deep down, Barry had all the motive in the world to murder his own wife.

I decided to pay Barry a visit despite Arthur's objections and went to his house. It may not have been the best idea at that time, but I needed answers, and I needed them fast. I saw that his police cruiser was in his driveway and parked right next to it. I got out of my car and plowed through overgrown vegetation to get to his weathered front door. There were patches of weeds and tall grass everywhere. I inspected further and noticed that his roof was missing shingles. The exterior paint of the house was faded and peeling. Barry had severely neglected his house after Caroline's death.

I took a deep breath and knocked. I heard a garbled shout from inside and patiently waited. Barry soon swung open the door. I almost gagged because of a rank odor that wafted out from inside. He looked at me up and down. I remained steady and kept eye contact.

"Venus? Venus, Venus, Venus. What are you doing here?"

"Hey Barry. How are you?"

He took out a cigarette and lit it. He took a puff and blew it in my direction. It took every fiber of my being to *not* kick him in the balls.

"Why would you give a shit?"

So this is how it's gonna be.

"You're my brother-in-law."

"My brother doesn't even talk to me anymore. We don't talk either. Why are you here?"

"He wants to talk to you again."

Barry came out of the front door and closed it. He folded his arms and glared at me.

"Where the hell is he then? Why did he send his wife? What kind of pussy shit is that?"

"He was afraid you were gonna try to fight him if you saw him."

"Damn right! I should fight him. I should kick his ass for what he said to me. Sorry Venus, I mean no disrespect. It just pisses me off. It's something between brothers."

"I get it. Look Barry, he doesn't want to fight you. He wants to hang out. That's all. He wants to take it one step at a time."

"Why the hell would I believe that?"

I remained quiet and stared at the floor. I didn't want to say it, but I had to. It was the only way, and it was for them.

"He realized that life is short. He uh—, he realized that after my family was murdered," I said softly.

Barry's eyes strangely lit up when I said that. It boiled my blood. Why did he seem so excited?

"Now that was nuts. The *St. Devil Beheadings.* They really killed your family and cut off all their heads. I wonder who did it. That was some crazy serial killer shit."

"How often do you wonder about that?"

"I don't know. I wonder about a lot of things. Why? Do you have a problem with that?"

Once a piece of shit, always a piece of shit.

"I have no problem," I said, fighting back the rising irritation in my voice.

Barry always found a way to cause issues or to argue. For as long as I knew him he had been doing it flawlessly.

"I think you do. I think you wonder about it too."

Shit.

My heart raced as he got closer to me. I remained still.

"What are you talking about?"

"I heard you've been talking to the neighbors."

"Where'd you hear that?"

"I'm a cop. We hear lots of things."

"I was just inquiring about Walter's disappearance. That's all. I report true crime. It's my job."

"Ah, that's right. You make your little videos with the creepy music, and you have the little promos. I remember seeing one about an air fryer. It reminded me of Caroline..." Barry trailed.

"She used one a lot?"

"No, I wanted her to get one, but she fought me on it. Now she's gone and I bought one for myself. It's funny how that works, huh?"

"Yeah, that's funny."

What the hell is he going on about?

"I miss Caroline, you know? We used to fight a lot, but I miss her. It makes me think..." Barry threw his cigarette butt on the floor and smushed it, extinguishing the small orange light.

"What do you think about?"

"I've been alone for a while now. I could use some company. Good things don't happen to me when I'm alone. I don't know what to do with myself. I don't know what to do with my thoughts. Caroline used to know. She tried. She always tried."

"Being with someone is good. It's important. I know that when I lost my family, I would've lost my mind without Arthur. I don't know what I would've done."

Barry suddenly gripped both of my arms and leaned forward. Sheer rage churned in my stomach. If he didn't let me go in five seconds, I was fully prepared to kick him in the balls.

"Venus, I want to see Arthur. I want to talk to him. Okay? I need to see him."

"That's fine. That's what he wants."

Barry let go of me and sighed. I quietly joined him.

"We're gonna have a great time." Barry smiled.

"I don't doubt it."

"Do you wanna come to my garage? I have my other car in there. It's black. I'd like your opinion on it." Barry grinned.

Is that a threat?

"I should really get going. I'll talk to Arthur okay?"

"Yeah, you do that. I'll drink a few beers with that asshole." Barry threw back his head in uproarious laughter.

As I fast-walked back to my car, I only thought one thing.

What have I done?

I sat in my living room with my hands clasped together, anxiously waiting. I stared at the clock and counted each click, one by one. It reminded me of the throbbing red welts that formed on my back whenever my Father felt I needed a punishment. He would viciously whip me with a leather belt. I only wanted to escape the house for one night. I had been trapped with a cruel, violent monster for so long. All I wanted was to taste freedom for a few hours. Not if he had something to do about it. He was like a shadow. He pounced on me just as I gently turned the knob of the creaky back door.

"Where the hell do you think you're going at this hour?"

"I'm just...I don't know."

"You don't get to leave here without permission. I'm going to make sure you never forget that." Father cruelly whispered.

Thwack. Thwack. Thwack. Thwack.

My mother wasn't able to do anything about it because he always made sure to lock the door. She was forced to hear my bestial screams as my Father violently struck me with complete ruthlessness.

I rarely allowed him to hit Vera like that. I saved her whenever possible. I offered to take her "punishment" myself. She was too young and too fragile. If any young girl could take it, it was me. If I had one thing to thank my Father for, it would be for shaping me into the type of woman who didn't stop for anything or anyone. I endured. I was hellbent on finding the truth and in finishing what I had started. People called me stubborn, but I called it holding myself accountable for the victims and loved ones who deserved justice. The ones who deserved to be remembered and to be delivered the truth, even if they were dead. The people who were alive would know. I would know.

Caroline had been shot in the face with a shotgun. It was a gruesome murder. The police reported that the shotgun's barrel was most likely placed in her mouth when the murderer pulled the trigger. It was downright brutal and macabre. The upper half of her head had been completely blown off. Brain matter, pieces of her shattered skull and broken skin had exploded everywhere. I couldn't look at the crime scene photos without vomiting. They should've never been leaked. But I had to look, at least once. I reported on it with teary eyes. I knew Caroline fairly well. She was my brother-in-law's wife after all. She was a beautiful, kindhearted woman who deserved to live out her years. Barry didn't deserve her.

I always suspected that Barry had something to do with her murder. He was an unstable person and a police officer at that. A highly dangerous and potentially murderous cocktail mixture. Barry was a rowdy drunk at family parties, and we never liked him. I tried my best, but he was insufferable. He would go on misogynistic rants about how women needed to go back to their motherly roots to stay at home. According to him they needed to solely birth children and provide food for the family every day. Caroline always looked at him with great contempt. Her dismayed face always said it all. I only wonder why she stayed with that lunatic.

One time, Caroline had told Barry that most women were able to balance motherhood with a career. That was enough to set him off and we were forced to intervene as he was getting too physical. When I saw that Caroline was on the verge of tears, I almost punched him in the face, but Arthur beat me to it. He shoved him down and told him to stop. Barry was bigger and taller than his older brother, but Arthur wasn't afraid to put him in his place. My husband was normally laidback, but Barry's erratic behavior always brought out the worst in him. Whenever they argued, it was like they were turning back into little kids.

When the cause of Caroline's murder was believed to be a botched burglary gone very wrong inside a park, I never believed it. She had gone there very late at night while Barry had been asleep. There was obviously no camera footage and no witnesses. No one apparently knew how poor Caroline had died. But there was one thing to consider. Caroline typically walked late at night to clear her head because of explosive arguments she would get into with Barry. I told the detective that when he questioned me, but they never followed up on it. They should have investigated the marriage between them more, but since he was a cop...there was bias, even if they stressed that there wasn't.

A sworn protector of the law would never kill his wife.
Barry loved Caroline more than anything in the whole world.
If he actually killed her, we would've caught him by now!

I didn't know if Barry could be the serial killer or not, but I knew that there was no love lost between him and my family. He was an extremely disturbed individual, and the possibility of multiple killers was possible. For all I knew, Walter was either dead or a potential killer. David, Caroline, Walter, Violet, Vanya, and Vera. All victims of tragic and mysterious circumstances.

It was insane that I wanted Arthur to be alone in the same house as him. I tried to convince him of coming up with another plan, but he insisted. He told me it was his brother and if things got bad...Arthur had brought a gun. I didn't know if he had the balls to pull the trigger, but Arthur was determined to go. He wanted to do what was necessary, but I knew the truth. Arthur was not a killer. There was no going back. I tried to convince him to forget about it, but he knew that I'd go back myself. He was right about that. I was adamant about finding the killer. Besides, I told Barry that Arthur would visit him. If he didn't go that would look very suspicious. We didn't want Barry to pay *us* a visit. Especially after he apparently shot at me.

I jumped and my heart skipped a beat when Arthur stormed through the front door. He was flustered and shaking. He paced back and forth while anxiously running his fingers through his hair. I sprang up and went to him. I grabbed his arm. He stopped and looked at me with frightened eyes. It was a rare occurrence to see him in such a frazzled state.

"Arthur, what happened? What's wrong? Talk to me." I commanded.

"He...he did it," Arthur whispered.

"Did what?"

Arthur's mouth opened but no words came out. He was trembling and his eyes started to water.

"Barry..." He murmured.

I softly guided him to the couch and sat him down. I held onto his arm and tried to get him to look at me.

"Arthur what happened? Tell me. You're scaring me."

"We...we should be afraid. I found...everything, Venus. *Everything*."

My heart was beating so fast I thought it was about to shoot out of my chest. My worst fears had been realized and the anticipation was about to kill me. I needed to know.

"Arthur! Tell me what happened!" I shouted, trying to break him out of his trance.

He blinked rapidly and finally met my eyes. He grabbed ahold of my hands and softly nodded.

"I did what you told me to do. I went over there, brought drinks, and got him drunk. We watched the basketball game on his TV while he drunkenly confessed to it all. I couldn't believe what I was hearing. I knew he had done some bad things but this...this was evil. I don't look at him as my brother anymore. I see him as a spawn of the devil."

"Oh god. Did you record it?"

Arthur took out his phone and scrolled through some applications until he got to **Voice Memos**. He pressed play on the first voice recording and put it on speaker.

"Dude, Walter's an idiot. He totally fucked Violet and probably got caught. I wish I could've had a turn. That's why he's missing. That

dude fled the country. But yeah, he used to buy coke off me. He was a fucking animal. He secretly hated his life. We're not that different. I wished I could've had a turn with Vanya and Vera too. Ha! Well, we know what happened with Vanya. I don't wanna get pepper-sprayed again. Can you believe she thought I was gonna rape her that one time? She wanted it. It's not rape if you like it. Everyone knows that. Caroline wasn't even home. It would've been fine. I was gonna kill her eventually anyway. Walter always had the right ideas about that. Ha! I'm just fucking with you dude. If I shot Caroline I might as well have shot Violet, Vanya, and Vera too. Get that quadruple kill like in those shooter games we used to play. I should've chopped off Caroline's head too. It would've kept things the same. A nice little pattern. Lord knows she deserved it for always fucking nagging me. Holy shit man. She was the biggest bitch ever. You don't know how many times she pissed me off. I'm glad she's fucking dead. Good riddance. I finally got some quiet around here. You know I'm just kidding with you, right? This is all bullshit I'm talking. I'm a little drunk but I'm good. I want another drink though. Talking about Caroline pisses me off. I'm happy we're talking again, bro. I missed you."

The recording ended and Arthur closed the app on his phone. He silently cried and quickly wiped his tears. I hugged him and rubbed his back.

"My brother's a monster. He's not human. He can't be," Arthur mumbled.

I felt like throwing up but did my best to maintain my composure. Barry disgusted me to no end but after that recording, I wanted to puke my guts out. He was absolutely revolting. The way he talked made me so angry I wanted to punch a wall. But I couldn't act out. He was my husband's little brother. I needed to stay strong for him.

"I'm sorry, Arthur. I'm so sorry. I wish he wasn't like this."

Arthur pulled back and gripped my shoulders. He tried to slow his breathing.

"When he fell asleep, I did it. I went inside his room. It was a huge mess. I ransacked the place. I found black gloves, black trash bags, shoe covers and black masks. Stuff that leaves behind no DNA. One thing about Barry is that he always kept weird pictures in his lockbox, dating back to high school. I never told you. He kept photos of dead cats, dead fish, roadkill, and squashed bugs. He had one in his room with the same code, his birthday. I found horrible photos. They're one of the worst things I've ever seen. I didn't want to, but I took a few pictures for evidence."

Arthur went to his photos on his phone and showed me what he found. They were blurry pictures of different women with different colored hair. One was dirty blonde, one was brunette, and one had pink hair. Their faces were completely blown off and bloodied. A mangled mess of crushed brains, shattered bones, red flesh, and detached eyeballs.

"Is...is that...is that them?" I said breathlessly.

"It's them. Barry is the serial killer. My own brother is a sick murderous monster. I'm related to a monster."

He took those pictures before slicing their heads off. What a sick son of a bitch.

"Oh my god."

He reluctantly showed me one picture that had my face on it with a red cross drawn over it.

"I think he wants to kill you next," Arthur whispered.

A violent stream of stomach bile immediately erupted out of my mouth. The anxiety-riddled, burning sensation in my gut had been too much to bear. I had to let it all out.

CHAPTER 10
5 YEARS EARLIER

I remember the first time I saw Barry drunk. The majority of the events in that memory were a bit hazy, but I fully remembered my interaction with *him* that night. It played in my head like a crystal-clear video. Arthur's family had invited me to a birthday party that took place in a banquet hall. It was a formal event with a spacious floor that had several dining tables with floral arrangements and bottles of champagne. A massive, central chandelier hung from the high ceiling and provided an aesthetic of pure elegance. The atmosphere was loud and festive with energetic party music blasting.

I did my best to keep my inner butterflies at bay so I could attempt to have a good time. I wore a silky black dress and a pair of black high heels. I did my nails and my mascara. It was one of the few times in my life where I felt really good about myself. When Arthur saw me, he smiled brightly. My heart swelled and I felt the heat rising in my rosy cheeks. I was by myself at the bar area which was located in a far corner of the room.

"Hey Venus, you look gorgeous. Wow. I can't believe you agreed to be my girlfriend."

"Me neither." I smirked.

We both giggled. I hopped off the barstool I was seated in and came closer. He wrapped his arms around my back and leaned in. He planted a soft, passionate kiss on my lips which sent an electric, tingling sensation down my spine and throughout my body. When we pulled away, we held on, and we couldn't stop smiling at each other.

"You wanna know why I love you?" Arthur asked sweetly.

"Because this dress is showing off my legs?"

"That's one reason, but the other one is...I admire you, Venus. You're a brave person and you're so stubborn. You get things done. I love that so much about you. You know what you want, and you don't let anyone, or anything get in your way."

Little does he know that on the inside...my fears and my anxieties threaten to cripple me almost every day. I'm just really good at hiding it.

"Thank you, Arthur. I think I love you even more for saying that out loud. I guess this is the part where I tell you what I like about you."

"It can be." Arthur chuckled.

"Well...I got nothing."

Arthur scoffed and was about to pull away when I forcibly yanked him back in. I grabbed his face and kissed him deeply.

"Wow. I really felt the love there." Arthur smiled.

"I love you because you're always gonna be there for me. You're dependable and you're my rock. I know you're not going anywhere."

"I'm not, but how do you know? How are you sure?"

"Because I told you everything that was wrong with me and you're still here," I said, squishing his cheek.

"I'll always be here."

Suddenly my phone rang. It was Vera.

"I'll be back. My sister's calling."

"I'll be here."

I exited the room and came out to the hallway.

"*Hi Venus. I'm sorry to bother you. I know you're at the party.*"

"*It's okay, sweetheart. Is everything okay?*"

"*It's just...dad's angry. He got into a fight with mom and threw something at her. I think it was a vase. I tried to help her by giving her a band-aid, but dad yelled at me to get away from her. He picked me up and pushed me against the wall. I ran away to my room. I'm really scared. I just wanted to know if you could pick me up. I don't wanna be here anymore. If you can't that's okay.*"

My heart sank as a ball of fury raged in my stomach. I wanted to bash my Father in the head with a hammer to get rid of him forever. The violent thought quickly dissipated. There was no way I'd be able to do anything against him. He'd kill me first.

"*I'll be home in 10 minutes, Vera. Just stay in your room and try to stay calm, okay?*"

"*Okay Venus. I love you sis.*"

"*Love you too.*"

I hung up the phone and needed to rush back inside. I needed to tell Arthur that I was going to leave early. Before I could do anything,

I was cut off by Barry who was clearly drunk. He stumbled in front of me and creepily smiled at me with squinty eyes.

"*Heeeeey* Venus." Barry cooed.

"Hi Barry. I don't wanna be rude but I really gotta find Arthur then get going." I tried to get past him, but he suddenly snatched my arms and leaned forward, his face inches away from mine. Panic began to set in, and I was fully prepared to kick him in the balls if necessary.

"You look so good tonight. Why do you look so good, Venus? My brother sure knows how to pick them huh?" Barry squealed with laughter. I wasn't amused.

"Let go of me, Barry. What's wrong with you?" I struggled to go free, but he wasn't budging.

"Wait, wait, wait. What's wrong? We're talking. I'm just *taaaaaalking* to you."

Vera was waiting for me. I didn't have time for Barry's bullshit.

"You have five seconds." I warned.

"Oh my god, Venus. Why are you being like that? It's a party. Let's have some fun baby. Let's go dance. Let's get groovy." Barry's hands slipped over to mine as my skin crawled. He rocked them back and forth like a swing. I dug my nails into the palms of his hands, and he flinched away.

"Ow! What the hell?" Barry grabbed my arm again but that time I shoved his hand away and kicked him squarely in the balls. He cried out in pain as his eyes bulged out of their sockets. He collapsed to his knees and held himself as he groaned. I went over to him and forcefully grabbed his shoulder. I squeezed it until I felt bone.

"Ow, ow, ow, ow, ow. Please stop, please stop, please stop." Barry begged.

"Do something like that again and I will tell Arthur. He'll have another reason to hate you. You piece of shit."

I grabbed a fist full of his hair, pulled it up and pushed him down to the floor. I was *pissed*. A volcanic-level ring of fire was rapidly circling my heart. If Vera hadn't needed me, I would've dragged Barry to the police station myself. It was a good thing I didn't. Looking back, I'm shocked at the fact that Barry hadn't gone after me. When I learned of his severe mental issues, I counted my lucky stars that he didn't murder me after what I did to him. He was definitely fantasizing about it...and I gave him a reason to.

PRESENT DAY

Arthur and I told the police everything. We showed them the pictures and had them listen to the voice recording. They already knew about his unstable nature due to him working with them. That was a disturbing revelation.

Everyone seemed to suspect that he had been involved in Caroline's murder, but nobody was able to do anything about it...until that day.

I stood on a wooden chair in an empty warehouse to look out of a small rectangular window with my binoculars. I diligently watched as the police secretly prepared to raid Barry's house down the street. They had advised us to stay away from him and to stay home but I had to see. Like the Kenneth Kilhouser raid, I had to see how it all ended. Arthur stayed home with a bottle of whiskey. He was prepared for the worst.

A SWAT team of a dozen officers were huddled together in a straight line, cutting through the front yards of the houses that neighbored Barry's. They carried assault rifles and ballistic shields. Barry was considered armed and extremely dangerous. They weren't taking any chances.

They were rushing in through the side so Barry wouldn't be able to see them coming from his front window. They didn't want him to be alerted before they got there. Once they arrived at their destination, they rapidly surrounded the house and formed a perimeter. The lead officer knocked on the door and waited for a response.

Barry! Come out with your hands up! We don't want this to end badly. You're one of us! We have you surrounded! Don't try anything funny and we'll all get out of this alive! He shouted.

First I heard a sharp crack followed by a powerful boom that sliced through the air with a deep roar that reverberated throughout the entire neighborhood. The shotgun blast shattered a window and dented a few ballistic shields. Barry quickly managed to shoot one of the officers in the leg. The shot shredded through bone and blew it off. His gurgling scream was so loud it sounded like he was right next to me.

Another volley of shotgun blasts went off as the two warring parties exchanged fire. It sounded like a warzone. I had instinctively ducked when I heard the relentless gunfire piercing through the quiet air. It completely disrupted the peace the neighborhood was in.

When I slowly rose and poked my head back up, I saw a shotgun blast rip through an officer's helmet. It obliterated half his head and killed him instantly. I gagged and closed my eyes for a brief second before I continued to watch the insane chaos unfold. The SWAT team members in the back of the house finally managed to break in and rushed inside, guns blazing.

Just as they entered, Barry dived through one of his broken front windows and threw his shotgun at the officers. He pulled out a handgun and fired away as he desperately attempted to escape. He let out a guttural scream which was quickly cut short. He got littered with hundreds of bullets, ripping through every inch of his body until he was a bloodied, lifeless mess on the ground. I closed my eyes and sighed. It was over. I descended from the chair and sat on it. I bent over and hung my head low. I slowly breathed in and out.

It's over, Venus. It's over. He brought it upon himself. He's a murderer and a sociopath. A brutal, inhumane, heartless serial killer.

When I got home, Arthur was already drinking. When he saw me, he stood up from the kitchen table and stared at me in anticipation. I slowly shook my head. He hung his head and sat back down. A few tears rolled down his cheeks as he rubbed his head. I sat down beside him and put my hand on the back of his neck, trying to comfort him.

"Why did my brother have to be evil?"

"I don't know, Arthur. I wish I did."

I looked down at my belly and gently rubbed it.

"What now?"

"We wait to hear from the police. We'll know more when they conclude their investigation," I said.

"I've been meaning to ask...the bullet holes on your car...what happened?"

"I'm pretty sure it was Barry. A truck was following me at night and then shot at me. It looked like his pick-up. I was waiting to tell you. I'm so sorry."

"No. I'm sorry." Arthur wrapped his arms around me and sobbed.

"What the hell did my brother do?" He sobbed.

All I could do was hold him. I couldn't tell him the dark truth. Barry was dead... and the world was a better place because of it.

We might've been wrong. Barry wasn't the suspected serial killer as far as we knew. But he did murder his wife. The forensics team at the St. Devil police department found traces of Caroline's blood all over his house and in his pick-up truck. It was concluded that Barry had shot and killed her in their own house. He then placed wigs that matched the hair colors of my mother, Vanya, Vera, and myself on Caroline's head. Since Barry was a deeply troubled individual, it was assumed that he was acting out some sort of depraved murder fantasy. In other words...he was a fucking lunatic.

Shocker.

They found a notebook that belonged to Barry as well. It had disturbing scribbles, drawings, and ramblings about killing women. He wrote about *ending* my mother, Vanya, Vera, Caroline, and myself. The police figured that he planted Caroline's dead body at the park himself along with the empty shotgun shells. What they didn't find was evidence of Barry actually murdering my mother, Vanya, or Vera. They didn't find an axe, traces of their DNA or their severed heads. They were at an impasse as they couldn't question a dead man. Regardless, they continued to search the house and any connection he had to the *St. Devil Beheadings.*

When will all of this end? If Barry's not the serial killer, is he still connected somehow? Is my Father connected to him? What about Walter? Where was he? Dead? Alive?

There was at least one thing that Barry seemed to confirm. That my mother had cheated on my Father with Walter after all. What other secrets did Walter have?

CHAPTER 11

We held Barry's funeral service at a community park with a large field. Arthur was at a podium near his casket along with three members of the Honor Guard. Since Barry was a veteran and a police officer, he received the three-volley salute. This meant that the Honor Guard would fire blank cartridges out of their rifles into the air to signify duty, honor, and sacrifice. I scoffed at the idea. There was nothing honorable about Barry. He purged himself of that moral when he blew his wife's head off with a shotgun.

I had half a mind to set fire to the flag that was draped over Barry's casket. It was ironic. The same people who killed him were the same people honoring him. There was about ten rows of ten foldable chairs that were formed in a square-like shape in front of Barry's casket. It was filled with police officers and military veterans who had known Barry. None of Barry's family members went, not even his parents. Only Arthur was there, ready to close the chapter on his little brother.

"As you all know my little brother Barry is gone. He was a very troubled person who suffered from severe psychological issues due to his service in the military. He was an army veteran, and he was stationed in Kunduz, Afghanistan for two full tours. He unfortunately sustained PTSD while he was there. I know the story all too well. It'll haunt me now more than ever before. He was on patrol one day and was riding through a village with his unit. Out of nowhere the military transport in front of him was blown up and destroyed. Four of his friends turned to ash just like that. They didn't even have time to grieve or fully process what had happened. They were immediately shot at, and hundreds of bullets whizzed by Barry's head as he dove for cover. Many of his friends who he considered his brothers were killed that day. Miraculously, he was not hit. But he was scarred for life. The horrible incident tormented him for days and nights on end. He was never the same after that horrific ambush and life never became easy for him. I wish things were different, but they aren't. I'm sorry I couldn't do anything to help you, little brother. You weren't perfect, but I'll still miss you forever. All I hope now is that you're finally at peace and that life is easy for you again, wherever you are." They briefly clapped.

The Honor Guard turned, aimed at the sky, and fired three shots. As Arthur made his way through the crowd, he hugged many veterans and police officers who offered their condolences. I found it very strange that Barry was receiving such a warm reception after brutally murdering his own wife and his own fellow officers. I waited for him a good distance away near a softball field where there was quiet and space. I knew that's what Arthur needed. When he got to me, I embraced him for several minutes. When we let go, I noticed Arthur's misty eyes. I wiped it for him with his handkerchief.

"Thank you. I couldn't have done this without you." Arthur sighed.

"Of course, you're my husband. You also did it for me not too long ago."

I put my arm through his and we went for a walk away from everyone.

"I felt like a fraud up there, but I couldn't mention Barry's murders. He's dead already. Should I have mentioned it? Am I wrong?"

"There's no easy answer for that. He's your little brother. It's hard to call him a bloody murderer at his own funeral. It is fucked up though. He killed his own wife and he wanted to kill my family. He fantasized about it. Who knows? Maybe he did kill them. We'll have to wait and see."

"Poor Caroline. Her parents didn't come obviously. You saw the messages they sent me. They want nothing to do with me."

"It's understandable. They trusted Barry to protect their daughter and he turned out to be a psychopath."

"He should've never gone to the military. I told him so many times. I was so worried and now look at what has happened."

"What's done is done. In the end, he made his own choices."

"I know. It's a tough pill to swallow."

I came to a halt and gazed at the sky. I wondered why I wasn't up there. I wondered why I had been spared a cruel fate. Sometimes I had dark, fleeting thoughts. Thoughts that included me wanting to be gone so I could join my family...wherever they were. Sometimes I felt like it was worse being alive. I was the only one left. I had to live without them. Could my fate be worse than theirs? I didn't know the right answers. All I knew was that I needed to go on despite what I thought or felt. I had Arthur and our baby on the line.

"Why are we surrounded by so much death?" I asked.

"I wish I knew."

"My Uncle David, my Aunt Vanya, Vera, my mother, Caroline, and Barry. All I have left is you and my Father."

"Your Father doesn't even count."

"He doesn't."

I stared off into space and closed my eyes.

"What are you thinking about?" Arthur asked.

"Death. What it must be like to live on the other side if there is another side. My mother, Vanya and Vera are all gone. I feel like I'm destined to be next. It's in my gut. It feels like a parasitic worm is gnawing away at my insides. Why should I be allowed to live? I feel guilty," I said.

"You'll survive this, Venus. We both will. I promise. You have to live for your family. Maybe...maybe it's time you put this to rest. Let's just move on from everything. We can start fresh." Arthur urged.

"No. I can't, Arthur. Don't even go there," I said shakily.

I didn't want him to try and convince me to stop searching for the serial killer that slaughtered my family. All he would end up doing is make me angry.

"Look at what happened, Venus. There was a fucking shoot-out at my brother's house, and he shot at you before he died! Something terrible could've happened. I don't wanna live without you."

"I'm not going anywhere, Arthur. I know what I'm doing, and I need to do this."

"This is all so dangerous. I worry about you, baby. I worry about our future. What if this turns into an obsession that never gets solved?"

"It will get solved. Stop saying things like that." I said angrily.

"We have to consider all possibilities. What other leads do you have now?"

"I know that Walter most likely slept with my mother and that he's missing. He has the key. Either he's the killer or he knows something. There's also the theory that David hired a hitman to kill Violet and Vanya because he hated them. I don't know how Vera factors into that, but she lived with Vanya. She was a witness that needed to be silenced. I guess," I choked out.

"That sounds like an insane conspiracy theory, Venus."

"Or it could be that David hired Walter because he's secretly a hitman. There's many possibilities. The mystery isn't solved yet, but I will find the truth."

"You sound like you're grasping at straws."

"Well, I'm fucking not so quit pissing me off! I'm trying, okay? I'm *trying*. This is my *family* we're talking about. The only family I had. The family that I *loved. Gone! They're all fucking gone! Forever!* They were fucking *butchered* like animals! They took them away from me! They fucking *robbed* me! My own family!" I shouted, my throat on fire.

Arthur came closer to me and hugged me. He gently stroked my hair. I was shaking as I felt my entire body flare up. My heart violently pounded in my chest and my breathing was shallow. I closed my eyes and told myself to calm down. If I didn't...I would've lost my shit.

"Okay, okay. I get it. It's alright. I just worry. That's all. You're my wife. I'm with you."

"I...I don't know what to do next, Arthur. After your brother...I just don't know anymore," I whispered.

"You have an entire platform dedicated to delivering true crime news and receiving true crime tips. I think you should use it." Arthur advised.

I vigorously nodded. I had almost forgotten about that. I hadn't looked at my social media pages in a long time. I had been so focused on finding the serial killer. Arthur was right. Someone out there knew something...*anything.* I quickly made a video updating everyone on Caroline's true murderer which was Barry. I then implored my followers to deliver any tips or information they had regarding the mysterious serial killer behind the *St. Devil Beheadings.*

At first I got nothing. There was a lot of trolling and dumb comments that had nothing to do with what I had asked. I almost deleted the video out of frustration until I received something nearly four hours after I posted the video. It was an email from an anonymous, temporary address.

It was a Google Images link. When I clicked on it, it was a large grassy field near a farmhouse and a forest. I zoomed in and leaned forward. I was trying to understand what I was seeing on my computer screen. When I realized what it was, I became brutally sick to my stomach and fell out of my chair. I was immediately dizzy and emptied out the acidic, burning contents of my stomach onto the floor. I hyperventilated as I clutched my belly and attempted to get to a normal breathing pattern. But it was no use. What I saw would haunt me for the rest of my life.

There was three elongated spears buried in the ground and on top of the three spikes were the bloodied, severed heads of Vanya, Vera, and my mother.

CHAPTER 12
20 YEARS EARLIER

I was considered clinically insane once. I didn't think so but that was the opinion of the doctors. The incorrect opinion I always used to say. From 5 to 15 years old I was admitted into a psych ward several times, on and off. It was called the Harrington Psychiatric Institute. What a hell hole that was. It was because of the physical and mental abuse I suffered from my horrid Father. I would draw pictures of scribbled monsters on several pieces of paper and would hang them all around my room. Each and every one would say *MY FATHER IS A MONSTER*. I was only trying to speak the truth, but no one ever believed me. I knew my mother did, but she never admitted it. She sided with him out of fear and because he paid for everything. When I told the doctors that my Father would whip me with a leather belt and other objects, they didn't believe me. They thought I had an overactive imagination. They didn't believe that my Father was a psychopath who wanted me to "obey" him at any cost.

To everyone else, he was a wonderfully charming gentleman who told clever jokes and inspiring stories about his early business struggles. For the longest time I didn't understand why they never believed me. I had the evidence. They came in the form of bumps, bruises, cuts, and welts.

The psych ward was a cold, dark place that greatly depressed me. The dim lighting, the inedible food, the stiff hospital bed, and the grey, prison-like walls only served to make me hate my life. The worst thing was the lack of freedom. I couldn't do anything without being watched, supervised, escorted or "helped." I had to force myself to behave well so I'd be discharged. Whenever I would go back home from the psych ward, I'd get sudden anxiety attacks whenever I saw my Father. It was like a giant hand was slowly closing itself into a fist around my heart. My mom had to give me medication so I would calm down. It was the only thing that allowed me to function like a normal person, which I hated. I didn't want to be dependent on pills. I wanted to feel and act normal all on my own.

School was the toughest. I didn't trust anyone, and I was always on edge. I had a crippling fear towards older male figures. One time a male teacher touched my shoulder in the hallway to greet me. Alarm bells went off in my head as I felt a vicious, primal instinct activate within me. I turned and before I knew it, I was on top of him. I was attacking him and trying to pin him down to the ground. I got suspended for that incident. My parents were furious. My Father had been forced to pay an undisclosed sum of money to keep that teacher from pressing charges against me. Apparently, I almost scratched his eyes out.

In the psych ward I came to know a woman named Dr. Minghella. She was a kind, soft-spoken lady with beige skin, curly brown hair, and glittering eyes. I liked her very much because she brought me snacks that didn't taste like dogshit and talked to me about the monsters I drew in my prison cell.

"Why do you like drawing these monsters, Venus?" Dr. Minghella asked as she gave me some small packages of Oreos.

"It's my way of showing the truth of who my Father really is."

"But your Father is kind and generous."

"That's his mask. You haven't seen him without the mask."

"What is he like without the mask?" Dr. Minghella grabbed a few strands of my hair and started brushing it with a comb.

"He's a monster."

"Could you be more detailed?"

"I've already told everyone a million times. He whips me with a belt, he hits me with a metal stick, and he calls me horrible names. He's a monster!" I shouted.

"Venus...is it possible that this is in your head?"

"What are you talking about?"

"Could this be a way of you attributing your self-imposed injuries to your Father?"

"Self-imposed? These are not self-imposed. I don't hurt myself, Dr. Minghella."

"Okay, fair enough. But what about the pills?"

"What pills?"

"The Furaprofen."

"I'm not taking that."

"You were taking them. You were abusing them."

I looked at Dr. Minghella with a very perplexed expression on my face. I never abused those pills. I knew I was in a psych ward, but I swore that I wasn't crazy.

"How do you know that?"

"Your mother told us, and she showed us the empty bottles."

"The only thing I take are anxiety meds that she gives me."

"Are you sure?" Dr. Minghella asked.

That was when I realized. My mother had been duping me the whole time. She wasn't giving me anxiety meds; she was giving me pain pills.

"My mom said I was abusing painkillers?"

"Yes."

"That's insane."

"She lied, didn't she?"

"Yes."

"I had suspected for a while that you didn't belong in here. I'm glad I was right."

It was absolutely unbelievable. I immediately figured out what they had done. My parents spun a false story that I was abusing pills and self-harming to cover up the real story of how I got my injuries. My mother was trying to protect my Father and as usual he was out for himself. I was forced to live a lie for years and had to admit to being someone I wasn't. Dr. Minghella said it was the only way I'd get out early. Sadly, they found out that Minghella had told me things she shouldn't have so she got transferred. I was all alone yet again. I always had to think on my feet in my family. I knew that if I didn't, I would die.

CHAPTER 13
PRESENT DAY

When I saw the severed heads, Arthur had been there. I didn't hide my reaction. I couldn't. It was too brutal. I told him what I had seen, and he quickly agreed to come with me. He refused to let me go by myself. I sensed something evil coming our way. I only hoped we would make it out in one piece.

He drove across the lonely one-way road that was adjacent to the entirety of farm country in St. Devil. They called it Devil's Orchard. We were heading towards the estimated geographical coordinates of the severed heads. I knew there was a strong possibility it was the serial killer that sent me that anonymous tip, but I didn't have much of a choice. I had to risk it and follow the trail, wherever it led. Besides...I already knew who it was.

"You really think it could be him?" Arthur asked.

"Only my dad would torture me like this."

"If you say so."

"My Father is the serial killer. It has to be him."

"What about Walter?"

"I don't know. He's missing. He could be an accomplice or out of the picture."

"Remember, he slept with your mother. Who knows, maybe he killed her because she threatened to tell Sandra or Dennis," Arthur said.

"That wouldn't explain the murders of Vanya and Vera."

"Maybe they found out too. I don't know. I'm just spit balling. Walter is a wealthy guy. He has a lot to lose."

"My Father is the serial killer, Arthur. He is the only person I know who would do something like this. Plus, he had an axe when I was younger. I know he did. I just couldn't find it," I said.

"Okay, so if Dennis does turn out to be the serial killer, what then? What will you do?"

"I'll end him forever."

"Understandable. But I mean when it's all said and done."

"Are you seriously hinting at having a baby? At this time?"

"No, no! I swear I'm not. I'm just talking about you. What are you gonna do to get past this? If it turns out your Father is a serial killer who murdered your mother, aunt, and sister...how the fuck are you gonna deal with those demons?"

"I...I don't know yet."

It was a valid question. I had no clue what I was going to do. First I had to see if my instincts from the very beginning were true. I had to find out if my Father was the serial killer or not. Barry and David were suspicious candidates that could've been involved in my family's murders, but I decided to cross them out. The police got back to me about Barry potentially being the killer behind the *St.*

Devil Beheadings. They strongly believed that he wasn't involved. At least there was that. Walter still wasn't off the hook.

"Maybe you should go back to therapy." Arthur suggested.

I immediately became defensive.

"I'm not going back to that shit. It didn't help me."

"You weren't consistent with it, babe."

"I don't like talking about all my shit with some stranger. It was weird and she wanted me to go into detail. I'm not going into detail on how my Father used to rip the skin off my legs with a metal stick." I cringed.

"I get it baby. I wouldn't wanna talk about that either. What about medication?"

"You're out of your fucking mind. I'm never taking that stuff ever again. That crap pretty much ruined my life for ten years."

"But why, Venus? Why haven't you told me? Why do you keep it a secret?" Arthur asked, concern washed over his face.

"Never again, Arthur. My life will not be destroyed by monsters!" I shouted.

I buried my face in my hands and cried. The crushing weight of losing my family, the abuse I experienced from my Father, it was all too much. The darkness I felt in my heart had spilled out. I couldn't contain the grief anymore. I had to let it all out. Arthur freaked out and pulled over. He put his arms around me and held me for the longest time as I doubled over into my own stomach.

"Venus, what's wrong? What's happening? Do you need anything?" Arthur asked frantically.

I glanced up and shook my head. He was my rock, my stable place and the one person who knew me best.

I just need you to stay here with me and to never let me go.

He deserved to know, and it was high time I told him. I sat up and wiped away my tears. I grabbed his hands and held them tight.

"You know about my dad hitting me and my sister when we were younger."

"Yeah. You told me."

"Well, I kind of sugar-coated it. It was way worse than what I told you. It wasn't here and there that he'd slap me or spank me. He would shove me against the wall, he would kick me in the shin, he would pin me on the floor with his hands wrapped around my throat, he would pull my hair until it felt like my scalp was on fire and he would whip my back with a leather belt until I had welts the size of a rock and skin lashes that were six inches long." I explained.

"Jesus Christ, Venus. I'm so sorry you had to go through all of that. That must've been so painful. That is so fucked up. I mean, coming from your own Father..." Arthur trailed.

"The big secret though...the one I've never told you is that...I was in and out of a psych ward from the ages of 5 to 15 years old. My Father told the doctors that I was self-harming when in fact, he was the one causing all the injuries on me. They never believed me, and my mother never told them the truth. She helped cover up my Father's violence to save him. It was easy to deceive them. My Father is charming, funny, and kind when he wants to be. He has no criminal record and runs a very successful business. They don't know him like I do. They don't know that behind that mask is a cruel, sadistic psychopath who abuses his own family. He's the monster in all my nightmares."

Arthur's face twisted into a mixture of profound sadness and anger. He took a few seconds before saying anything.

"My god, Venus. I had no idea. I hated your Father before but now...oh, I fucking loathe him. I can't believe I had dinner with him and acted kind to him. I can't believe I fished with him. I'd kill him if I had the chance," Arthur said darkly.

"I know you would, but don't be a monster like him. You're so much better than that and I love you for it."

Arthur brought my hands close to his lips and kissed them.

"You're so strong for getting through all that and still being the most wonderful person I've ever met."

"I don't know about all that. I'm broken, Arthur. I have been for a long time."

Arthur gently grabbed my face and turned it to his. A fire was blazing in his eyes. Something I had never seen before.

"Hey, you are *not* broken. You never were. You are brave and so strong for surviving your evil Father's abuse. You could've easily lost yourself to nothingness, but you got through it. You survived, Venus. You survived ten years in a psych ward. You can get through anything."

I gazed at him as my heart gushed with an overwhelming amount of warmth and love. I leaned over to him and passionately kissed him for several minutes. When I pulled away, he laughed.

"What was that for?"

"For making me feel better." I whispered.

"Anytime."

I wanted to tell him about my pregnancy but hesitated. I was still worried he would try his hardest to pull me off my manhunt. I didn't want him to worry. He had done enough for me. I was the one who needed to see it through to the end. I looked outside the car window and saw three small objects in the distance. I gasped. It was them. I quickly tapped Arthur and pointed. He turned and saw. We had stopped at the right place.

"Oh shit. It's them, isn't it? Sick bastard."

"We need to go. We need to go now."

"What if it's a trap or something? Nothing about this feels right. We need to be really careful."

"That's why you came with me and that's why we brought the sledgehammer," I said.

"My heart is in my throat, Venus. I don't know how you do this shit."

"I feel the exact same thing you're feeling. I just learned how to cope with it."

"Fuck it." Arthur swung himself out of the car and raced to the trunk. He brought out the sledgehammer and gripped it with two hands.

"Have you ever hit anyone with that before?"

"No, but I almost hit my brother once. This is nuts, Venus."

"Trust me, I know."

We locked the car and quickly jogged over to the three severed heads. As we got closer and closer, I could feel my chest tightening. It was them. By the time we reached the heads, I was on my knees, panting. The bloodied heads of Vanya, Vera and my mother were squarely fixed on three elongated spears that were buried into the ground.

"This is...this is pure evil."

When I got back up, I glanced once more at the chopped-off heads of my family. I sighed then took a deep breath.

"Ready to call the police?" Arthur asked.

We both saw him at the same time. A tall, menacing figure in the distance. He was strolling towards us. As he neared, I recognized him instantly. It was Father. I immediately took out my phone and called the cops. Arthur protectively stood in front of me with the sledgehammer raised.

"What the fuck is he doing here?" Arthur asked aloud.

"I knew it. I knew it was him. My Father is a serial killer. My Father is a fucking serial killer, Arthur."

"This is fucking insane."

"911, what's your emergency?"

"I need to report something immediately. I have found the severed heads of Violet Snow, Vera Snow and Vanya Reyes. Please track my location. I'm in Devil's Orchard. I'm on farmland. I have found the serial killer behind the St. Devil Beheadings. I repeat, I have found the serial killer that murdered the Snow family. It is Dennis Snow. It is

my Father. *He's coming towards us now. We think he's armed. Please send the police immediately!*" I urged.

"*I'm so sorry, can you please repeat who the severed heads belong to? Who is coming after you? The signal is spotty...*"

A fury rose in my gut so hot, I wanted to smash my phone on the ground. Time was of the essence and the spotty cellphone signal could potentially cost us our lives.

"*It is the detached heads of Violet Snow, Vera Snow and Vanya Reyes. I have found the serial killer that the police have been looking for in St. Devil. I repeat, this is the St. Devil serial killer who murdered the Snow family. The serial killer is Dennis Snow. I am Venus Duarte, his last remaining daughter. He's coming after me and he will kill me if you don't fucking hurry!*" I shrieked shakily.

"*Help is on the way ma'am. Try to stay as far away from him as possible...*"

I hung up the phone and stood my ground alongside Arthur.

"What do we do?" Arthur asked, his voice trembling.

"I don't know."

"I...I have my gun in my back pocket."

"Okay. That's good."

"If Dennis does anything funny, you take it and you shoot him." Arthur commanded.

"Are...are you sure?"

"If he tries to hurt us, we have no choice. Right?"

I heard it in both of our voices. We were both unsure, but I had to be the one to make the choice. It was my own dad after all.

"Right. I'll do what I have to."

He abruptly stopped. He took out his phone and appeared to be reading something. My phone rang an alert, and I urgently checked it. It was another anonymous email.

"Dig out the spot on the ground with the X. You'll find what you've been looking for. You'll find the truth."

"What is it?" Arthur asked.

I spotted the X and quickly went to it, dropping to my knees and digging out the dirt until I felt solid objects.

"Another anonymous email. It told me to dig here to find the truth."

"Oh god. What was buried?"

I felt a solid wooden handle and slowly took it out of the ground. Dirt was caked all over it, but I managed to wipe off most of it. It was an axe. The presumed murder weapon.

"Oh shit. That's it. That's the murder weapon. There it is."

"We'll see."

I continued to sift through the ground. I found a wallet, a broken phone, and a silver ring.

"What is that stuff?"

"I don't know. I think it belongs to someone."

I opened up the wallet and checked if it had an ID. It did. It was Walter's driver's license. I almost dropped it in shock and showed Arthur.

"Walter? Your neighbor? Oh shit. What the hell is going on?"

"Is Walter dead?" I thought aloud.

"I don't know but Dennis is starting to walk again."

I continued searching. I felt something round and cold. When I pulled it out, I immediately screamed and threw it aside. I was instantly disgusted as goosebumps erupted all over my body. I went towards Arthur and grabbed his shirt.

"What? What was it?"

"It was a pair of human eyeballs. It looks like it's been cut out from someone's head." I gagged and tried my best not to puke.

"What have we gotten ourselves into, Venus?"

"I have no idea. I'm sorry, Arthur."

We heard dozens of police sirens in the distance. Soon after, we saw police cruisers roaring down the road, speeding towards us by cutting through the field. Father reached us before they did.

"Looks like you got here before I did," Father said gravely.

"I knew it was you this whole time. I fucking knew it."

"I have no idea what you're talking about," Father replied.

"*Yes you do!*" I shouted with utter ferocity.

"I assume that you're here because you also received the photo link and the message to dig into the ground with the *X*. Am I right?" Father asked.

A sense of uncertainty and confusion bubbled in my stomach as an army of police officers descended on us.

What sick games are you playing?

CHAPTER 14
18 YEARS EARLIER

It was only a matter of time before she found out about my psych ward hospitalizations. My parents couldn't keep it a secret forever. It was another famous family gathering at my house.

It was David's birthday and Father made sure to throw the biggest extravaganza he could. There was live music, a mini-bar and over 40 people celebrating the occasion in the backyard of our house which had an infinity pool with a custom-built rock waterfall. There was also a full outdoor kitchen with a built-in hybrid fire grill and a long marble patio table that seated over 20 guests.

While guests heavily drank, danced, and obnoxiously laughed throughout the entire yard space, I took Vera to the front yard. It wasn't a place for kids and guests were inside the house too. My anxiety increased tenfold whenever we had that many people in our house. I couldn't breathe and felt like there was a stormy cloud over my head, ready to pour down at any second.

I had just been released from the psych ward for the umpteenth time and was not in a good headspace at all. All I wanted to do was spend time with Vera. I hadn't seen her in months. I helped her ride her bike as my Father never wanted to take the time to teach her. I held onto the handlebars with her as she coasted around the neighborhood.

"Why do you keep leaving? Where do you go?" Vera asked innocently.

"It's uh—, it's a place where I can get better."

"Get better from what? Are you sick?"

Yeah, sick in the head. Apparently.

"It's just a place to be alone. You know how I like my alone time."

"Venus! That's so sad."

I couldn't help but giggle aloud. My laughter infected her, and she started squealing with joy as well. That was the only therapy I needed.

"It is pretty sad, isn't it?"

"Promise you won't leave again. Please. I don't like it when you're gone. Mom and dad fight so much. It's scary."

I stopped her and softly held her shoulder. She looked up at me, expectantly.

"Does he put your hands on you? Be honest with me," I said sternly.

She shook her head.

"No. I do what you told me to do. I hide when he gets angry, and I don't talk to him. I pretend like I'm a ghost."

"Good. You know why you have to do this right?"

"He's the monster from our nightmares. We have to stay away."

I put my arm around her and squeezed.

"You might just survive little sister." I muttered to myself.

We both turned our eyes to the front of the house as a smiley Vanya came stumbling out with a glass of champagne in her hand. She floated over to us with outstretched arms and hugged us both so tightly we couldn't breathe. When she let go, she massaged Vera's hair while she leaned towards my ear.

"I know you're not in a behavioral program or temporary boarding school. Your parents are hilarious. I'm going to kill Dennis." Vanya whispered.

"What do you mean?"

"Don't worry, sweetheart. I'm going to handle it."

When the party was over, I found Aunt Vanya and my Father arguing in the backyard near the pool. I hid behind a boxwood bush to eavesdrop.

"Why the hell is Venus being admitted into a psych ward?! She's not crazy!" Aunt Vanya yelled.

"You don't know anything about the situation. Stay out of it." Father commanded.

"I know enough. They're stuffing her full of pills in there and they're going to kill my little girl if you don't stop!" Aunt Vanya warned.

"She's not your little girl." Father murmured.

"She should've been." Aunt Vanya scowled.

"Vanya, you're talking nonsense." Father rubbed his forehead and went to go sit on the edge of the pool with his back turned.

"If you took her out, she would recover from whatever illness you think she has. Vera misses her too. She needs her sister."

"She draws horrible monsters on paper and tapes them all over her room. She says it's me. She says I'm the monster from her nightmares. She has major mental issues, Vanya. I don't touch that girl."

"Why would she lie about that?"

"Lie about what?" David entered the backyard and wasted no time inserting himself into the conversation.

"Fuck off David. This is private."

David glared at Vanya. He was probably thinking up ways of cutting up Vanya into little pieces. They had no problem expressing their hate for one another.

"Our dear Vanya wants me to take Venus out of the Harrington Institute."

"What? Vanya, you have no clue about the situation. You have no business telling Dennis how to manage his daughter when you have no child nor husband."

Vanya's mouth gaped open, and she scoffed.

"You are one rude son of a bitch. You know that? Everyone thinks you're so quiet and timid but you're not. You wait until your big brother is around to talk shit. That's when you start running your mouth," Vanya said, her voice shaking.

"You can say whatever you want. I know what you are. You're a greedy hog and you tried to sleep with Dennis before he started dating Violet."

I saw Vanya's face turn boiling red as she marched over to David and slapped him as hard as she could. David stumbled back and rubbed his cheek. Father quickly stood and went to his brother's side.

"You don't know what the hell you're talking about," Vanya growled.

"I do know. Brothers tell each other everything," David said with a smirk.

Vanya slowly approached David, but Father cut her off. He icily stared down at her. He was a giant compared to her. David hid behind Father and smiled to himself. That summed up their entire relationship. Big brother always protected little brother.

All they had was each other growing up. That was the harsh truth about them. Their parents were neglectful and rarely present. Drugs, drinking and all the other usual horrible shit. Father made sure to guide David throughout those confusing, tumultuous years. He fought off bullies and deflected girls trying to take advantage of David's intelligence in school. Father had been a popular athlete due to his natural gifts. He was tall, fast, and strong. He had all the makings of an efficient, deadly serial killer. David was quiet but observant. He was the ghost in the halls who heard the gossip and the whispers. He reported anyone talking badly about them to Father. Father took care of them quickly. He found out early on that violence was a deadly weapon that intimidated and instilled fear into those who wanted to see him fail.

How did I know all this? My mother told me. She fell for his charm and later realized what he really was. She found out through his actions and through the stories he would tell her. She figured out that Father used to punch his classmates into submission if they so much as called him "freak." My Father and David were quite the duo. The truth was...I believed the both of them had the urge to kill within them all along. All it took was tragedy to ignite it.

"What are you doing?" Father asked.

"What?" Vanya mumbled.

"Get out of here, Vanya. You've said enough."

"You know what I'm saying is true, Dennis." Aunt Vanya dared.

"You're testing my patience by continuing to talk." Father warned.

"How can you speak to me like that? I'm your wife's sister." Aunt Vanya shuddered.

Father leaned over and got in her face.

"I don't care who you are. If you speak again, I will break your teeth." Father threatened.

Aunt Vanya turned and stormed off. I caught a glimpse of her deeply troubled face. Aunt Vanya's eyes were watery, and her lips were trembling. I felt for her. I knew what it was like to be threatened by him. Father's words sent a cold shiver down my spine, and I felt like he would badly hurt me at any given moment. I was used to him shoving me, punching me, choking me, and pulling my hair. I hated him with all my heart.

"I wished she was gone. She's a poison to our family," David hissed.

"She's a silly little drunk. She gets emotional. Leave her be."

"All I'm saying is that I don't think anyone would miss her if she was dead," David said bluntly.

Father nodded and tapped him on the shoulder.

"I understand perfectly."

"If only..." David trailed.

"If only..." Father echoed.

An ominous sentence that was never finished. The air was always charged with an uncomfortable energy that filled me with anxiety. I felt no peace. I felt like something terrible was bound to happen at any given moment. Unfortunately I was proven right on more than one occasion.

"I need to tell you something. I've seen Violet speaking with Walter outside your house, many times."

"How have you seen that?"

"I keep an eye on things."

"Always the observer, huh?"

"You know me best."

"That's very creepy, David. When I told you to get out more, this is not what I meant. You're behaving like a stalker." Father chuckled.

"You need to keep an eye on Violet and Walter. I'm serious."

Father strolled over to the sliding door that led inside and peeked through the glass. He turned and held his hands up.

"I don't see Walter in there, but if I find him in my bed I'll let you know."

"This isn't a joke, Dennis. I'm trying to look out for you."

"I know you are. I appreciate it."

"I don't trust them, especially Walter. He's hiding something."

"You don't trust most people."

"You trust too many," David shot back.

"I don't. I just pretend to." Father winked.

"Should I talk to Walter? I can ask him about *Violet's Vagina Elixir*." David mused.

"I told you about that?"

"Of course you did. You told me she only tells her lovers about that drink. It's a lemonade."

"A very good lemonade. It's reserved for Violet's lovers. No one else can drink that drink."

"So do I talk to him?"

"Don't worry about Walter. He's harmless." Father patted him on the back.

I lost my footing and accidentally grazed the bush with my elbow. I gave myself up by making a ruffling sound. I frightened myself and started to crawl backwards on my back.

"Who's there?! Who's listening?! Vera?! Venus?! I better not see you!" Father boomed.

I got up and ran as fast as I could towards the front of the house through the wooden side gate. I closed it shut and made my way around to the front door. My heart was pounding, and I was short of breath when I saw my mother smoking a cigarette. When she saw me she looked at me with shame in her eyes. She threw her cigarette on the floor and put it out with her foot. She bent forward and stretched out her arms with a warm smile. A rare sight. I slowly entered her embrace and hugged her. She softly rubbed my back and kissed the top of my head.

"I'm sorry about sending you to a mental hospital. It wasn't right. I let your Father convince me and I shouldn't have. I had doubts but...he can be so persuasive. Vanya was right. You need to get out. She'll help me. Your Father will give in. You've been in there too many times. It's time to come home."

Tears rolled down my cheeks as the shock electrified my entire body. I hadn't experienced kindness from her in years.

"If you do take me out, please tell Dr. Minghella. She was the only nice person there."

"Don't worry, I will tell her." She promised.

I don't remember if my mother ever did tell her. I never saw Dr. Minghella ever again after I officially left the Harrington Institute. My mother had kept her promise despite my Father fighting tooth and nail to keep me in. He made me promise to never call him a monster ever again. He also commanded me to never draw those "horrible little things" inspired by Satan. I promised, but I did draw those horrible little things. I drew them in my mind. That's where the nightmares resided anyway.

CHAPTER 15
PRESENT DAY

"You're wrong, Venus. I'm not what you think I am," Father urged.

"I don't fucking believe you. Not for a second."

"Venus, the police are coming," Arthur warned.

"I got the same message you did! I'm innocent! Don't you see what's going on?! They wanted us to find each other and to blame each other! Whoever killed our family is playing games with us! They're manipulating you!" Father shouted.

My head was spinning, and I was sick to my stomach. I had no idea what to believe. I began doubting myself. I knew my Father's true nature, but something about him being there...didn't seem right. I was doubting myself, but he had to have done it. I strongly considered that there was an accomplice.

"What's your game?!"

"What?"

"You did this! I know you did! Who's helping you?! Is it Walter?! Is he dead?! Why did you kill all of them?! Why?!"

Father shook his head and dropped to his knees while putting his hands behind his head.

"You're confused, Venus. I know I'm a lot of things, but I'm no killer. I loved them all...and I love you...despite what you believe," Father said softly.

Before I could respond, the police officers closed in and shouted at us to get on the ground. Once they spotted the three severed heads of my dead family, they drew weapons.

Everyone down on the ground now! Hands behind your head!

Arthur immediately dropped the sledgehammer and laid down on the floor with his hands behind his back.

"Shit. This is bad," He whispered.

"Wait! No! I'm the caller! I'm the one who called! I'm Venus Duarte!"

"Down on the ground now!" An officer tackled me to the floor and put handcuffs on me as I struggled to go free.

"You've got the wrong idea! I didn't do this! I called this in! Get off of me!"

"Don't you dare hurt her! Don't hurt my little girl!" Father bellowed.

"Please don't hurt her! She's the one who called you guys!" Arthur shouted. He tried getting up, but three officers pinned him down and pointed their guns at him. They dared him to move.

"Don't move a fucking muscle," an officer warned.

Arthur froze and did what he was told. Eventually I realized that it was a losing fight and gave in. They escorted all of us into different police cruisers where we all took the long ride to the police station. The rest of the police unit formed a perimeter around the scene of the severed heads. I kept my head down and tried to relax. I needed to get my story straight. I was at a secluded location where there was three chopped off heads on display like trophies. There was also an axe, the alleged murder weapon. Not to mention, Walter's belongings mysteriously buried into the ground. Belongings that I dug out myself. The first sign of him since his disappearance. It didn't look good at all.

"It was an anonymous message that I received. I swear." I told the detective. He softly nodded and jotted down notes on a tablet. I was in an ice-cold box of a room with metal chairs that made my butt sore and lifeless white walls that reminded me of the psych ward.

"Why didn't you immediately call the police?"

"I wanted to see what it was first. I called the police pretty quickly once I realized it was the three heads of my murdered family," I said.

"Got it. Now, why did you say that your Father was the serial killer over the 911 call? What led you to that conclusion?"

"The fact that he was there at the same time I was. That's obvious enough, isn't it? He's playing with me. He wants me to know it was him and he knows I can't exactly prove it yet. That's how sick he is."

"Well, there you go. You said it yourself. You can't prove it. All you have is an inflammatory accusation based on a gut feeling."

"It's not inflammatory. He's my Father. I know him. It's the truth!"

"I'm sorry Venus for your losses. I really am. I can't imagine losing so many loved ones like that. Look, we're done here and you're free to go."

"Thank you, detective."

"I'll walk you out."

"What about the axe? Is it the murder weapon? What about Walter? Walter's wallet, broken phone, wedding ring and a pair of eyeballs was buried there. Is Walter dead? Did he do it?"

"Thank you Venus for giving us the scene and for helping us locate vital evidence that relates to the case. We think this is going to be a big breakthrough in finding the serial killer behind the *St. Devil Beheadings.* Hopefully we can give you the closure you're looking for."

The detective practically pushed me out of the room. I stomped out of the police station, pissed. I needed information. I needed to know what was going on with my dad too, but they refused to tell me anything. I was reunited with Arthur not long after I was released. We hugged each other outside the police station, and I kissed him like I hadn't seen him in years.

"That was nuts," Arthur said.

"I agree."

"We're never doing that again."

A ball of anxiety formed in the pit of my stomach as I softly shook my head.

"What do you mean?"

"Venus, that was insane. We found the heads, an axe and Walter's stuff. There's something really fucking sinister going on. Plus, your dad was there. It didn't even seem real. What the hell is going on?"

"What do you think I'm trying to figure out? This is why I've been searching for the truth, Arthur. Look at what we found. That place was a depraved burial ground and a tribute site. That was the marking of the deranged serial killer. They wanted me to find that. My Father wanted me to find that."

"I don't know, Venus. Why would he be there at the same time as you? I think whoever messaged you, messaged him too because you're both apart of the Snow family."

"He was there because he was watching and waiting for us. He's playing mind games with me. He always has."

"You said that place was the marking of a serial killer...what if it was Walter? His stuff was buried there along with an axe. What if that was his way of saying it was him?" Arthur suggested.

It was plausible. I had to give him that. It was very odd why his things would be buried unless he was also murdered.

"It could be him. There was no head but there was a pair of eyeballs."

"What could that mean?"

"It could mean he wanted us to see or bear witness or something. Serial killers love leaving behind cryptic messages like that."

"Whatever it means, I think you should take a break and lie low for a while. That was a fucking terrifying situation. That was the most intense thing I have ever experienced. I don't want you to be in danger like that again."

"That's why you came along."

"I shouldn't have agreed. That was batshit crazy."

"This whole situation is batshit crazy. A serial killer chopped off my family's heads with a fucking axe."

"I know."

"An axe was at that place. It could be the one that sicko used!"

"I know Venus. All the more reason to lie low and let the police do their jobs."

"I don't trust the police."

"We're talking in circles." Arthur sighed.

I didn't want to argue anymore. We were at a stalemate and neither side would budge.

"Fine, I get it. I'll lie low for a bit. I need a break." I lied.

"Thank you. That'll keep me calm."

"Let's get out of here before the press show up."

"They're still trying to talk to you?"

"To my Father."

Arthur suggested I meet with a therapist, so I did. I talked with a Dr. Perez and by the end of our session, I wanted to throw her out of a window. She seemed very familiar, but I couldn't put my finger on it. She seemed to know me too. I laid down on her L-shaped couch as I stared at a ticking wall clock that seemed to grow louder and louder by the second. The room was dark and cold. There were Rorschach paintings on the walls and strange sketches of squiggly lines and colors. I felt like I was in an asylum. I felt like I was back in the Harrington Institute. The same feelings of dread and anxiousness filled my stomach like a balloon that was ready to pop at any given moment. Dr. Perez sat behind her solid oakwood desk as she urged me to spill my guts out. She was a petite woman with green highlights in her hair and silver horn-rimmed glasses.

I didn't tell her everything but enough for her to know that I had been through a very tough time.

"So you didn't have the most pleasant childhood growing up, correct?"

"That's right. It was uh...it was pretty bad."

"Why is that?"

"Why do you need to know?"

"I'm only trying to help you, Venus. That's why I ask the hard questions. It's my job."

"My Father didn't treat me well. Okay? He was an asshole. The biggest one of them all. That's all I'll say."

"I understand completely. What about your mother?"

"She was kind of an asshole too. Less so than my Father, but...she had her moments. My Father affected her in a negative way. I think my Father's abuse was the reason my mother turned out the way she did."

"I see how that can be true. That makes sense, Venus."

"Thanks, for believing me I guess."

Dr. Perez adjusted herself on her chair and cleared her throat. She looked at me and smiled. I grew uneasy.

"Well, Mrs. Duarte, here is my professional opinion regarding this whole situation. It is my belief that you created an aspect of your Father in your mind that is the serial killer that murdered your family because...you needed him to be."

I was in complete disbelief. Why the hell would I make up my Father being a serial killer?

"I don't understand."

"Your Father unfortunately abused you when you were a child. You drew him out to be the monster that haunted your nightmares and for this reason your parents sent you to a mental institution. They feared that you were mentally unwell because they claimed your Father never laid his hands on you."

Anger was rising in my chest like lava building in an active volcano.

"Oh that's bullshit! He did hurt me! He fucking hit me like there was no tomorrow! I had the bruises and everything!" I exclaimed.

"The doctors at the institute concluded that they were self-inflicted."

"Yeah, I know. It was bullshit. Why would I hurt myself like that? Tell me, Dr. Perez, why the hell would I ever do that to myself?" I asked fiercely.

"You were mentally unstable, Venus."

I felt like storming out of there right then. I couldn't take it any-more. I was used to hearing complete nonsense regarding the grossly inaccurate history of my hospitalizations, but Dr. Perez was really grinding my gears. I took a deep breath and closed my eyes for a second. Then it hit me.

"Wait...how do you know that I was sent to a mental institution? I never told you that."

"I figured you didn't recognize me. I knew you didn't want to reminisce about that tumultuous time in your life. I was one of the doctors that handled your case, Venus."

The pieces of a blurred memory played in my head. That's why she was so familiar. She was one of the doctors who worked at the Harrington Psychiatric Institute.

"I remember now. Why did you ask me about my childhood then? You already know most of what happened."

"I was assessing your memories because you're an adult now and it was a long time ago." Dr. Perez explained.

"Do you know how Dr. Minghella is? Is she still working?"

Dr. Perez couldn't look me in the eye and was squirming in her seat. She ran her fingers through her hair and clacked her pen against her clipboard.

"Dr. Minghella doesn't exist."

I stood up and shook my head.

"No. No, no, no. What are you talking about? Dr. Minghella helped me. She helped me a lot."

"It was a chaotic time for you, Venus. You created Dr. Minghella in your head and talked to her when you were alone. She was your imaginary friend."

"Imaginary friend? Are you serious? That's—, that's nuts. I don't believe that."

"We went along with your delusions because we were observing your mental health and behavior. I'm sorry, Venus," Dr. Perez said.

I paced the room as I struggled to breath. Dr. Minghella wasn't real. I couldn't believe it. I had been talking to myself. When I thought back to that time in my life, it almost made sense. I never remembered Dr. Minghella entering or leaving my room. She would always just appear out of thin air and then disappear. I never saw her talking to the other doctors and never saw her outside of that room. I knew deep in my heart that Dr. Minghella wasn't real, but I had refused to accept it. I didn't want to think of myself as a crazy person. A crazy person never thinks of themselves as crazy though.

Dr. Minghella was the only person who made me feel like I was normal. I didn't feel like I was spiraling out of control or losing my mind when Dr. Minghella was there. I felt at ease and at peace. I wondered if I was only able to be at ease inside of my own mind, away from the outside world. The idea frightened me. The nights after my Father would torment me and leave behind a storm of violence in his wake. It made me want to fall into a deep sleep and never wake up. Somehow I found the strength to keep going when I found myself awake and still breathing.

"It's...it's okay. I see it now. It's what I had to do to survive. Dr. Perez, what do you think being stuck in a place like that does to a person?" I asked.

"I always hope that it rehabilitates a person. I want my patients to get better and to live happier lives. That's the end goal of any doctor."

"It didn't rehabilitate me. It made me feel like I was a fucking lunatic. In reality, I probably would've been way better off not going there ever in my life. You know what would've rehabilitated me? My Father not existing. By the time I was able to escape him, it was too late. The scars he left were stuck inside me and they were cut very deep."

I started towards the door as Dr. Perez remained silent and only stared with shocked eyes.

"We don't have to finish the session. You can still keep the full amount I paid you. Thank you for your time, Dr. Perez."

I didn't care if Dr. Minghella had turned out to be a figment of my imagination. I knew that my Father did abuse me. I didn't make that up. I had the lifelong wounds to prove it. The ones you didn't see. The ones that faded away over time but stayed in your mind. I was in my bedroom, scanning through various news articles and headlines regarding our arrests on my laptop. I had gotten a few requests for interviews but hastily declined them. I had no interest in speaking with a bunch of sleazy, sensationalist reporters. However, my egocentric, psychopath of a Father loved talking with those reporters.

I wasn't surprised when I saw that he had been released. I clicked on the video and watched in disgust as he reveled in the attention he was getting.

"*Mr. Snow why were you arrested?!*"

"*Is true that you have connections to the serial killer that has been terrorizing St. Devil?*"

"*Is it accurate that you were sent an ominous message by the serial killer himself?*"

My Father was able to silence everyone with a simple wave of his hand. He drew them in with his eyes and addressed them like he was the President of the United States. I rolled my eyes so hard, I thought they were about to fall out their sockets.

"*Hello ladies and gentlemen. I hope everyone is having a fine afternoon. My arrest was just a huge misunderstanding. A case of being at the wrong place at the wrong time. I have a lot of properties out west. As you probably know, there is a lot of farms and open land in that area. I happen to own many of those properties. I was doing a routine checkup when I stumbled upon a disturbing crime scene that I cannot comment on. The police have instructed me not to and I must respect their wishes. It's an ongoing investigation. They will give you more information when they are ready. Also, please note that I am certainly not a serial killer. I loved my family very much and I miss them every day. I may have divorced my wife, but I still had a lot of love and respect for her. I also miss my good neighbor and friend, Walter Campbell. I share*" *my grief with Sandra and with my remaining daughter, Venus. I only hope that we get the closure and the justice we deserve someday. Thank you,"* Father said with watery eyes.

He was escorted to a jet-black SUV by a security detail and promptly left.

Nothing but fluff and bullshit.

I continued scrolling through articles and found some that stated that the police believed Walter to be the serial killer and that he may have fled the country without anyone knowing. It was a plausible theory, but deep down I believed it to be my Father. Barry, Walter, and David all had skeletons in their closet. Father had the biggest one of them all. Maybe Dr. Perez had been right. I needed Father to be the serial killer. He was the monster from my nightmares, and I needed a reason to finally destroy him. Only then would I ever have a chance to be happy and have a family with Arthur. I gently rubbed my belly and for a brief moment, my heart felt full. It was warm and made me crack a wide smile.

"Don't worry baby girl or baby boy, mommy won't let you live in a world where Father is left standing. You will be happy no matter what. Whether you're alive...or not."

CHAPTER 16
1 YEAR EARLIER

Before Vera was murdered, I took her with me while I was reporting on the *Triple K Murders*. I took her off Aunt Vanya's hands because she wanted to *"be very irresponsible and get drunk at a bar."* I understood her. Once in a while you deserved the chance to enjoy yourself while fully knowing you were gonna regret it the morning after. It was called *living*. I wished I had gotten the chance years ago. I wished I wasn't robbed of my childhood.

We were driving through the seedier part of town on the way to *The Dirty Bin*. I was going to talk to Kenneth Kilhouser. At that time, he wasn't suspected of being a serial killer by the media. He was a victim. Kenneth's ex-wife, sister-in-law and daughter had all been slaughtered after all. It was his own family. I found it odd how he didn't seem to be affected by the tragedy though. When I saw his TV interviews his eyes were dead, and he displayed little to no emotion. I didn't suspect he could've been a serial killer because he had a solid alibi, or so I thought.

The night his ex-wife was murdered, he had been at a pool bar. He was cleared of the other two murders because he was shown to be at work. The alibi in regard to the murder of his ex-wife Diane was suspicious. I spoke with the workers who were there that night.

One of them claimed that Kenneth had left for 2 hours but there wasn't any evidence to support that. I was intrigued and wanted to investigate further. I knew that Kenneth owned a few laundromats. I decided to pay him a visit.

"So you think this Kenneth guy is the serial killer?" Vera asked.

"It's possible."

"Why do people kill?"

"What do you mean?"

"I get killing someone in war and stuff but why do some people kill like it's normal?"

It was an honest question, and I didn't have a clear answer for her.

"I don't know. Some people are really sick in the head. Or they kill because they're that desperate for money or drugs. Those people are the scum of the earth."

"The people who are really sick in the head freak me out. How do they get like that? How do they get so sick that they kill people for their own enjoyment or something?"

"I wish I knew the exact answer, but those people usually have very traumatic childhoods. So it's their way of getting back at the world for all the pain they've experienced. That's what I think anyway."

"We had a traumatic childhood. How come we're not murderers?"

I had thought about that when I became older and started reporting on true crime on a consistent basis. Many cases I reported on were eerily similar to my own. The killer had a tragic childhood marked by various forms of abuse and as a result, they turned out to be mentally deranged. I had my own issues as well. I apparently saw and talked to people that weren't there. I imagined things that didn't happen, and I had a hard time discerning reality from fiction sometimes. Despite that, I wasn't a killer. Why? Why didn't I choose to get back at the world for all the pain and suffering I went through?

As I looked deeper within myself, I eventually learned the answer.

"We're not murderers because we had each other."

"That's really sweet of you to say."

"Well, think about it Vera. We saved each other. You saved me when you were born. I wouldn't have survived if I had stayed alone. I tried to save you as much as I could growing up in that violent shithole."

"I'm really lucky I have a big sister like you. I love you, Venus."

Vera had a knack of bringing me to tears. I quickly wiped them away.

"I love you too, little sis. You're my shining star."

"I miss mom. I know she wasn't the *best,* but she tried."

"She always did try. I loved her for that. It wasn't easy. Not one bit."

"Have you thought about going after her killer?"

"I wish I could, but the trail ran cold."

"I wonder who killed her every day. I have no idea who it could've been," Vera commented.

Father.

"I don't know either."

"Do you remember that promise you made me about monsters when we were little?"

"What promise?"

"It was during a really bad night when dad was breaking stuff and going on a rampage. I asked you about monsters. You told me they only lived under my bed, but I asked you about dad. He was a monster that didn't live under my bed. He was a monster who bought me my bed and who tucked me in at night when he wasn't terrorizing us."

"I remember."

"I asked you if monsters ate us like in the horror stories you would read me sometimes. I asked you if they got away with all the horrible things they did. I thought they got to swallow us whole in the end. You promised me that they didn't."

"I promised you that monsters never win."

"Do you still think that's true?"

"I hope so."

We arrived at the parking lot of *The Dirty Bin* and found an open spot. We hopped out of the car and marched over. When we entered, I noticed it was a simple space with rows of washing machines and dryers. They were neatly lined up next to each other. I told Vera to take a seat while I slowly walked over to a long-haired, 40-year-old man with a scruffy gray beard who was at the far end of the laundromat. He was staring at a dryer as clothes tumbled inside of it. We were the only people inside. A fluorescent light was buzzing above him, illuminating him ominously.

"Hi. Are you Kenneth Kilhouser?"

He slowly turned his head and examined me with dark, haunting eyes. He looked like he hadn't slept or eaten in weeks. There were black circles around his eyes and his face was gaunt.

"Who's asking?"

"My name is Venus Duarte. I'm a journalist specializing in true crime."

"Who do you work for?" He coughed up phlegm and spat on the checkered floor like nothing. I hid my gagging and kept a straight face.

"I'm independent."

"Venus Duarte, huh? I think I know your Father...Dennis Snow. Are you his daughter?"

I rolled my eyes in my head and nodded.

"Yeah he's my dad. Snow is my maiden name."

"He's a very successful businessman. I look up to him."

"That's uh...that's good to hear."

"I'm only talking to you because he's your Father and I respect who he is." He pointed at me menacingly.

"I'm fine with that, Mr. Kilhouser."

"Good."

"May I ask you questions regarding the murders of your family?"

"Why do you report true crime?" Kenneth cleared his wet throat.

"I'm sorry?"

"I will ask my questions first, Venus. I want to know why you report true crime."

"Umm...sorry, I don't get asked that very often. I do it because I feel it's important to spread news and awareness about crime in St. Devil. The people deserve to know what's going on."

"That sounds like a bullshit answer. It's political. I want to know why *you* started reporting crime."

I had to stop my eyes from welling up with tears. I knew the reason why. There was only one. It was a tragedy. Abigail Flores was her name. She was my only friend in high school. The only girl I ever talked to. The others thought I was a freak because they knew that I had been in a mental asylum.

Don't talk to her, she's weird.

I heard she tried to kill someone.

That is one ugly ass girl.

She goes to the looney bin. Do you think she has two personalities?

Why would they let a crazy girl come to this school?

Those were a few hurtful whispers I had heard in the hallway. Abigail never said anything like that to me. She offered to sit with me during lunch and even shared her cookies with me. I was forever grateful for her friendship. She said something to me that would stick with me forever. We were in the courtyard in school, having lunch. The simple memory was ethereal. I saw a white mist surrounding us as we floated slightly above the ground.

"*Why are you so nice to me, Abigail? The other girls...they hate me. You don't. Why?*"

Abigail smiled and affectionately put her arm around my shoulder.

"I don't care about the rumors or the stuff I've heard about you. I make my own opinions. I always judge what's directly in front of me, regardless of what anyone says. Venus, you have a beautiful soul and you're stubborn as hell. I like that about you. You aren't a mental patient...you're one hell of a friend," Abigail said.

I missed her so much. It was only a few weeks later when tragedy struck.

"I...I report true crime because I lost a good friend who deserved justice. She almost didn't get it."

"What happened to your friend?"

"She was uh—, she was raped and stabbed to death."

"Who did it?"

"It turned out to be her ex-boyfriend, Robert Marwood. She had mentioned him a few times to me, and I told the police to look into him. When they didn't, I took matters into my own hands and exposed the texts she had sent me. There were detailed conversations that included Robert's angry messages and death threats. They finally looked into him after half the school went into an uproar. I gave them more information regarding his friendships and past romantic partners. They eventually found something. One thing led to another, and he was arrested."

"You didn't stop."

"How could I?"

"You really wanted justice for your friend. That's admirable."

"Thank you."

"You may ask your question," Kenneth said.

"How do you feel about the rumors floating around that you were the one who killed your own family?"

There isn't many, but I'll test him.

Kenneth chuckled and sucked in his teeth. He faced me and got closer to me. I stood my ground despite my heart rate increasing.

"I don't listen to town gossip."

"Do you have something you would like to say regarding those rumors?"

"Listen to me very carefully, Venus. I did not kill my family and even if I did...I wouldn't tell you, now would I?"

I was on the verge of a full-blown panic attack as Kenneth's intense eyes peered into my soul. I felt nothing but darkness emanating from him in waves. He was a truly disturbed individual. He was the type of man you would run from if you approached him on a dimly lit street corner on the wrong side of town. I had felt this before from someone. Someone I had known my entire life. My own Father.

"Thank you for your time, Mr. Kilhouser."

I quickly turned and fast-walked towards the exit. I grabbed Vera's hand and practically yanked her out with me. It took me mere seconds to get to my car. I jumped in and locked the doors as I began to breathe rapidly.

"Venus, what's wrong? What's wrong? Venus, tell me," Vera said anxiously.

I stuck out my hand and closed my eyes. She tightly clasped onto it.

"What did he say to you, Venus? Please tell me. Are you okay?"

I suddenly remembered the *Box*. I had flashes of being strapped and hit with a leather belt. I heard yelling and crying. I saw splotches of grey, brown and red. I saw a silver blade with a hilt. I remembered feeling so afraid that I was going to die. That happened to me more often than it should've.

As I opened my eyes, I felt my chest tightening. I rode it out and eventually experienced a calm release. I stopped breathing heavily and wiped my forehead which was thick with sweat.

"Sorry, I was freaking out for a second there."

"Oh my god, I was worried. What happened? Are you okay?"

"I...I think he's the serial killer."

"No way."

"He was very strange and intense. I know he's an outcast and a loner because of my previous research. I don't see why anyone else would murder his family."

"It's always the husband."

"It is."

"What are you gonna do about him?"

"I'm gonna take him down."

"Monsters never win." Vera stated.

"Monsters never win, little sis."

PRESENT DAY

I missed my little sister. She had gone through the wringer with me. If it was with her, I could do anything. I just felt reassured with her. I felt like she wouldn't judge me even if I failed. I was devastated at the fact that she would never get to meet her niece or nephew.

I was at the grocery store, shopping for the living resident who was growing inside my belly. It was a spacious building with a clean and well-organized interior. The layout was divided into different sections which included produce, dairy, meat, bakery, canned goods, frozen foods, and household items. I was checking some vitamin supplements when I saw him. A young man in a black jacket staring at me. I knew who he was, but I couldn't remember his name or where I knew him from.

I was shopping at night, and we seemed to be the only people in the store. I got what I needed and walked away from him. When I glanced back he was following me. I quickened my pace and turned the corner. I doubled back around the fruits aisle and pretended to look at apples. He came out and saw me. I tried to focus despite a knot twisting in my stomach.

I can't freak out. Not now.

I wasn't feeling the best because of the situation with Dr. Minghella. I couldn't believe she wasn't real. I was still having trouble with that. I didn't know what to trust in my own mind. I felt like I was going insane. I hated that so much. I had been in and out of a mental asylum for years. I couldn't actually be insane. Could I?

The man could've been a nobody for all I knew. I could've been freaking out for no reason at all. I closed my eyes and told myself to get a grip on reality. There was no way I knew that man. It was dark out and my mind was playing tricks on me. It was telling me that there was danger even though there wasn't any.

When the man came towards me, he nodded. I awkwardly nodded back. A surge of panic flooded my stomach as he grabbed a few apples and placed them inside a plastic bag.

"Have a good night."

"You too." I replied.

He strolled away and all the worry I had dissipated from my body. I had been losing it for no reason. He was just a man shopping for some apples.

Fucking apples.

I told myself to snap out of it as I went to the checking aisle. I paid for my things and left. When I went to my car to put my groceries away, I heard a soft whistle. I swiftly turned and saw him again. It was the man. He was quietly approaching me with a strange smile. I remained as calm as possible as I secretly took out my pepper spray and hid it in my hand.

"Hello."

"Hi," the man said.

"Can I help you with something?"

"Aren't you Venus Duarte?"

I hesitated.

"I am, yes."

"You're the true crime lady. You make those videos on social media. You promote those gluten-free, organic oatmeal shitpacks. Then you report that a young girl has been raped and murdered in her own home. Isn't that fucking funny?" The man smiled.

I need to keep my cool. This is clearly a whack job.

"I'm not very proud of those brand deals but...they allow me to spread awareness about these crimes. I show the people of St. Devil that they need to be vigilant. Some people even give me anonymous tips that I pass on over to the police. Sometimes it leads to arrests and justice being served."

"Sometimes it leads to people being killed."

I studied the man's face as he stepped a bit closer. I knew him from somewhere. I just couldn't remember. My mind was a whirlwind of conflicting thoughts and images.

"What are you talking about?"

"You got my father killed." The man took something out of his pocket.

"Wait a second. Who...who are you?"

In a flash, I screamed as the man suddenly rushed me and tackled me to the ground. I had no time to process the throbbing pain I had in my head. I used both of my hands to stop the man from stabbing me in the face with a knife.

"I'm Karl Kilhouser."

All the memories came flooding back. Karl Kilhouser. Kenneth Kilhouser's son. The son who had disappeared after his father was killed by the police. He had clearly come back with a vengeance. He blamed me for his degenerate father's death.

"Please...stop!" I urged.

"You got him killed. You're next." Karl growled.

"He killed your family." I said through gritted teeth.

"The voices told him to."

"You're just as sick as him."

I tried to knee him off of me, but he pinned me down with his legs as the knife got closer and closer to my face. Eventually it began to pierce my neck as I screamed in agony. The blood began to gush out and it spread all over my body. I began to lose consciousness.

"Now you're fucking dead." Karl hissed.

"I...I...I'm sorry." I choked out as I coughed up gobs of blood.

Suddenly the man's face changed. It was Vera. The blood was gone. It wasn't in my mouth or on my body. The knife wasn't in my neck. There was nothing but darkness surrounding me.

"Vera? What's going on?"

"I haven't seen you in a while," Vera said.

"I've been thinking about you lately."

"Did you catch him?"

"Who?"

"Our Father."

Tears immediately flowed out of my eyes as my lips trembled. I swallowed the lump in my throat.

"I thought I had him, Vera. I swear I did. I'm so sorry. I don't know what to do now."

"You know what to do. You need to keep going."

I looked at her in shock as she innocently stared into my eyes.

"What?"

"Look at everything you've been through. Look at everything *we've* been through. I'm dead now. I can't do anything...but you can. You can find the truth."

"How Vera? Where do I go from here?"

"You know what to do. Don't doubt yourself because they think you're insane. You know that you're not. Remember...our Father has a way of convincing you that he's right, but he's a psychopath. He does what he does best. He fools everyone and manipulates them. He puts on a mask and hides who he truly is."

"Okay Vera. I understand."

"Remember what you promised me...monsters never win."

"Monsters never win." I echoed.

I woke up in a pool of sweat in my bedroom. I got up and quickly grabbed a small towel from my nightstand to dry myself. It had been another bizarre nightmare involving Vera. I picked up my phone and disconnected it from the charger. I searched up Karl Kilhouser. He was still missing, and it was strongly assumed that he had fled across the border. I let out a breath I didn't realize I was holding and plopped backwards onto my bed.

Arthur's hand landed on my shoulder.

"I thought you were sleeping. I'm sorry if I woke you."

"It's alright. You're full of sweat. Did you have a nightmare?"

"Yeah, I did. I feel like a little kid."

"Hey, it happens. What was it about?"

"It was about Vera again. It was nice seeing her. I miss her so much."

I wasn't going to mention being murdered by Karl Kilhouser. I didn't want to freak him out. We had been through enough. If I had to take the mental suffering alone then so be it.

"Was she saying anything?"

"She told me she loved me and missed me. That was about it."

"I miss her too. I had a lot of love for her. She was the sweetest girl." Arthur kissed my arm then went back to sleep.

"She was."

Monsters never win.

It was time to keep my promise.

CHAPTER 17

I thought about the loose threads I still had. I had to figure out how it all connected. As I pursued my family's killer, certain clues had led me to Barry, Walter, David, and my Father. I wanted to go back to Sandra, but she closed herself off to me. She wanted nothing to do with me. Barry had spooked her good. Even in death, Barry caused problems for me.

I went back to David's old apartment to speak with the neighbor I hadn't spoken with. That was one loose end I hadn't investigated. I had to talk to Lee Smith. I remembered that he seemed to like lemons. I brought over two boxes filled with lemons, in hopes that he would be nice enough to talk to me. I held my breath as I knocked on his door. I heard indistinct yelling coming from inside. A full four seconds later, he yanked his door open and peered at me.

"What? What do you want? I'm not buying shit," Lee said with irritation in his voice.

"Hi Lee. My name is Venus Duarte. I have two boxes full of lemons here."

"Lemons? Really? Oh...well, I do like my lemonade. Who are you again?" Lee asked.

"My name is Venus. David Snow was my uncle. I just want to talk for a bit. That's all. I won't take up too much of your time." I pleaded.

"Didn't your family pass away? It was that horrible tragedy wasn't it?" Lee asked softly.

"Yeah. They were murdered," I said, a lump forming in my throat. I swallowed it and remained focused on the task at hand. Lee's facial expression softened, and he took the two boxes out of my hands.

"Thank you. Please come in and have a seat. I'll make us some cool glasses of lemonade." Lee stepped aside and allowed me to enter.

It was a neat place with dated furniture, old knick-knacks and display cases filled with medals. He had a couple of black and white portraits from a war. It looked like World War II. I found a torn couch and carefully sat down.

"You have a very clean place."

"Thank you. I do it for my late wife. She would've wanted it that way. If I don't keep things tidy, she'll come back to haunt me." Lee chortled.

"I'm sure she will."

Lee came over with two glasses of lemonade and handed me one. I took a sip and was pleasantly surprised with how tasty it was. It had a perfect blend of sweetness and sourness.

"This is very good, Lee. What's your secret?"

"My secret is my secret, lady. I say that respectfully."

"It must be one hell of a secret."

"Lemonade has great significance in my life."

"Why?"

Lee pointed to one of the black and white portraits.

"I am a veteran of World War II. I fought in Okinawa in Japan. My duty was the campaign in the Pacific. It was one of the most horrific jungles ever. I still hear gunshots, bombs and men dying to this day. Their screams were so terrifying. It never left me. You could never relax during that time. The moment you relaxed was the moment you were shot and killed. The Japanese were everywhere. Why was I talking about the war?" Lee asked.

"You were explaining why lemonade has great significance in your life."

"Oh, yes. The reason I love lemonade so much is because when I was in Okinawa, there was a local farmer woman who gave the US soldiers lemonade. She was afraid we were going to kill her. We promised to protect her, and we did. When the campaign was over, we gave her most of our rations and hugged her like she was our mother. We all sobbed like children. That lemonade got us through the worst of times. It eased our suffering by giving us something to look forward to." Lee explained.

"Something so simple seemed to save your lives."

"It did, Venus. I drink it now to remind myself of the brothers I lost. We fought in a terrible war. However, I realized that in the most horrific circumstances you can still find a single sliver of joy and hold onto to it for as long as you can."

"That's very well said, Lee."

I had been pleasantly surprised at what type of person Lee had turned out to be. I thought he was going to be a cranky old man, but he was thoughtful and genuine. He reminded me of everything my Father wasn't.

"I take it you want to talk about David Snow?"

"I do. How was he to you? How was your experience with him?"

"David was a well-mannered man who regularly asked me about my day. I had no problems with him or his brother, Dennis Snow. Dennis is quite the character. He's a very funny man. He's your Father, isn't he?" Lee asked innocently.

Yep. Unfortunately.

"Yes, Dennis is my Father."

"It's such a shame that David did that to himself. Such a big shame. I couldn't believe it, you know? I thought he was doing alright. It goes to show that you never truly know what's happening inside someone's head."

Tell me about it.

"That's what I'm trying to figure out. I need to know why David killed himself."

"You need closure for your uncle. I understand that. Unfortunately, I don't have much information that can help you. I'm sorry."

"Oh, I see. That's fine."

"Yeah, I mean—, I don't know. I told the police I saw that man arguing with David a few days before he died, but they never figured out who it was."

"Wait, what? What man was that?"

"I caught a good glimpse of his face when I checked outside my door, but I have no idea who it is. I even worked with the sketch artist, and they got nothing out of that."

"If I showed you a picture of someone, would you be able to tell me if it was him?"

"Yes, most likely."

I took out my phone and showed him a picture of Barry. He studied it and shook his head.

"Nope, not him. No way. That man has too many tattoos."

I scrolled through my camera roll and showed him a picture of Walter. Lee's eyes widened.

"Oh wow. That man looks very familiar. Wait a second...yes. I think that was him."

My heart started racing.

"Are you sure, Lee? You have to be sure."

"Isn't that the man who went missing?"

"It is. His name is Walter Campbell."

"I think it was him."

"Lee, you have to be sure it was him because I will pursue this as a lead."

"Venus, I can't tell you for a fact it was him because it was a long time ago. However, I strongly believe that it was him."

"That's good enough for me. Thank you, Lee."

David had been arguing with Walter a few days before he died. That was an interesting revelation. I spoke to Polly Westphal, and she also confirmed that she had heard two males arguing in the days leading up to David's suicide. I theorized that they were arguing because David wanted Walter to stay away from my mother. He had seen them chatting it up and was very suspicious. Walter refused but David persisted. So Walter decided to hire Barry to kill David and staged it as a suicide. The theory sounded very outlandish but at that point, there wasn't much to go off of. One hole in the theory was why wouldn't David immediately tell my Father? Maybe he wanted to wait until he was home from his business trip. Maybe Walter knew something about David that he didn't want anyone else to know. Barry would've killed David to feed his habits or to satisfy his violent urges.

"*I'm so sorry, but I had to do it. I hated you all.*"

There was also David's suicide note to consider. My investigation consisted of many questions and few answers. When I got home I scooped up a package that was resting near the front door. When I entered, Arthur was working in the living room.

"Hey babe." Arthur greeted.

"Hey, I'm happy to be home."

"Can I talk to you about something?" Arthur folded his laptop screen.

I nodded and sat next to him on the couch with the package still in my hand.

"Venus...do you really want to start a family with me?"

"Yeah Arthur, I do."

"I don't want it to feel like it's an obligation or anything. I just...I love the idea of raising a child with you. I think you'd be a phenomenal mother. I just don't know if you still want that after everything that's happened."

I felt like telling him right then and there, but I couldn't. The words didn't come out. They were stuck in my throat and refused to spill out. My gut told me it wasn't a good idea. Perhaps my anxious mind was playing tricks on me. All I knew was that I needed to solve the mystery behind my family's gruesome murders before anything else. I needed to see that through to the very end. The outcome of my personal manhunt would decide everything that came after.

"I want it. I promise." I kissed him to reassure him even if I wasn't sure what the future held for us.

"I can't wait. That package came earlier by the way. It has your name on it. I think it's from a brand or something."

"Yeah probably."

I got up and went into the kitchen to get a knife. When I opened the package, I immediately smelled a grungy, pungent odor. When I peeked inside, I gagged. I was cautious enough to hide my reaction from Arthur.

It was a man's private parts. It was bloodied and mangled. It had been chopped off. It was one of the most grotesque things I had ever seen. I quickly closed it and snuck out to my backyard. I didn't want Arthur to see. I figured that the serial killer was either taunting me or giving me hints. Both ideas made me sick to my stomach. If it turned out to be my Father, I swore I would not stop until he was *extinguished* from the world. First the eyeballs, then that...what was next? Someone else's head?

CHAPTER 18

I thought about it all day and night, trying to figure out what the body parts could mean. Eyes could mean to look or search around, but a man's private parts? I had zero clue. There was something that I couldn't remember that was stuck to the back of my mind like glue. It was like a bundle of words that were scrambled, and I couldn't fit them together.

I didn't want to go to the police. I didn't feel like I could trust them anymore. They thought I was insane. I was on my own. I stuffed the private parts deep into the trunk of my car until I figured out what to do with them. I thought about Walter. Was he toying with me? Was he the killer all along? Was I actually insane? No matter what I thought, I had to keep going. Only the truth would set me free.

I took a retractable knife and Arthur's sledgehammer. I drove through Devil's Orchard. The place where I was originally arrested and where I found the severed heads of my beloved family. It filled me with such hate and fury whenever I thought about a deranged psychopath slicing off the heads of *my* family. Whether it was Father or not, that psycho was going down. I refused to be next. I passed abandoned construction sites, storage facilities and farms on my way to the unknown. I searched through the vast, open fields to see if

I would spot anything strange. I wondered if I would find more detached heads on spikes. As I kept driving, I passed a street sign that read *Optic Drive*. I screeched to a halt. There were two silver screws at the top of the sign that made it look like a pair of eyes.

I gazed across to my left and saw an abandoned barn house. The paint was fading, there was a broken window, and the giant doors had a padlock. Everything around me grew still. It was so quiet all I could hear was the sound of my car humming and my own shaky breathing. A rumbling erupted in my stomach sending a shockwave of anxiety and fear throughout my entire body. The hairs on the back of my neck stood up and I started trembling. I rushed outside and violently puked onto the pavement. I bended down on one knee and tried to calm down. I massaged my belly and hoped that my baby was okay. I wasn't showing yet, but I would be soon. I knew I had to act.

I parked my car further up ahead near a clearing in the forest. It was well hidden as long as you didn't look too closely.

All the memories came rushing back the minute I laid my eyes on it. It was the *Box*. A difficult, very intense memory I had buried deep inside my mind for a very long time. A memory I never spoke about to anyone. A memory that I wanted to purge from my soul. I retrieved the sledgehammer from the trunk of my car and made sure that my knife was in my back pocket. I slowly inched my way towards the barn house.

I knew it was probably a trap and that there was a high chance I would die...but it needed to end. I couldn't wait any longer. If it was my time to die, so be it. I needed my life to be normal. I needed to sleep. I needed to live the type of life I always wanted to live with Arthur. Without the fear of something terrible happening to me. I needed to destroy the monster in my head once and for all. I needed to find the truth behind the serial killer who slaughtered my family. I had a strong feeling it would be done on that fateful, windy day.

I carefully climbed over the semi-high wooden fence as I approached the padlock on the door. I grabbed it and inspected it. It was rusty. When I let go, it clanged against the door. I stepped back a few inches and winded back the sledgehammer. I swung it high and fast against the lock. It clanked but remained firm. I winded it back again and swung even harder, mustering up all the strength I had. It broke off and clattered to the ground. My heart pounded in my ears as one of the doors creaked open. I slowly stepped inside while tightly gripping the sledgehammer. It was dark inside. I saw multiple stacks of hay scattered everywhere, as well as wooden barrels. It didn't look like anyone had been there for years.

I spotted a massive shape in the corner covered by a large black tarp. When I pulled it off, it was a car. A 1972 Firebird to be exact. It was Walter's car.

Alright, what the hell is going on?

I silently explored the entirety of the barn house while remaining on high alert. *Thump.* I staggered backwards as my heart almost leapt out of my chest. There was hay covering...something. I bent forward and used my hand to clear it. It was a rectangular, metal door with a latch. I pulled on it and it noisily grated against its hinges as I opened it. It was an entrance to some sort of cellar. It had a narrow metallic staircase that descended. I froze. It looked familiar.

Is this it? Is this where I die?

It was the dumbest idea in the whole world. I expected to go down a cellar that was underneath a creepy barn house and come out alive. I was insane, but I had no choice. I didn't know what was down there and I didn't know how much time I had left until someone came. But I knew I wasn't making a mistake. I knew that the *Box* was down there. A place I knew all too well. Before I went, I slid out my phone and sent Arthur a quick text message.

"Hey, Arthur. I'm so sorry for everything. I love you. I love you so much. I'm pregnant. I've been pregnant for a few weeks now. I'm so sorry for not telling you. I'm also sorry for not telling you that I'm in an abandoned barn house. I went after him, Arthur. It's near Optic Drive along Devil's Orchard. Please come and send help. Do not come alone. I know you probably hate me for doing this to you but there was no way I'd let you risk your life too. By the time you get here, I will know who the serial killer is. It's all coming to an end. It will finally be over. I love you Arthur. I love you more than you know. I know I'm fucking insane for sending this to you. I hope you can forgive me one day."

I had no idea if the message would even send due to the spotty signal. Regardless, I didn't plan on turning back. I didn't know if the serial killer had been alerted or not, but I didn't care. That was my one chance to see the truth. I needed to take it.

I took a deep breath and slowly went down with my heart in my throat.

Be strong, Venus. Be fucking strong. This is where it ends. This is where you find the truth.

When I made it down, I knew I had been right. It was a concrete box of a room with a pitched ceiling, rustic beams, and exposed wood. There was a magnetic silver wall with various knives, drills and other murder tools mounted onto it. At the top was an axe. The murder weapon that I knew existed. There it was in all its glory. A dangerously sharp, single-bladed killing machine with a long wooden handle. I frantically searched the rest of the room and found a body at the end. It was a man. He was chained to a wooden beam. As I got closer, I saw that he had a blindfold on. He was a dirty, bloodied mess. The man's hair was disheveled and haphazardly cut. He had tattered clothes and no shoes. Judging by how his shirt clung to his body he was dangerously thin. He reeked of urine and feces. He was breathing raggedly and didn't seem to realize that I was there. As I took a closer look at his face, I realized who he was.

"Walter?"

"Yes? Oh my god. Who's there? Who is that? That's not you, sir," Walter rasped.

"Mother of—, what the hell happened to you?" I tried to take his blindfold off, but he strongly turned away.

"No! Don't do it. It's no use. He took my eyes out. Who are you? Is he there?" Walter asked frantically.

He was almost unrecognizable. Walter was a paranoid mess of a man with a harsh, croaky voice. Who the hell knew what else this mysterious man had done to him. I immediately knew that Walter's eyeballs were the ones that had been buried along with his other belongings.

"I'm Venus Duarte. What happened to you, Walter? Who's the man who did this to you?"

Walter slowly raised his head and whatever was left of his eyebrows. He slowly nodded.

"Apparently you're his daughter," Walter whispered.

I felt my soul leave my body when he said that. My skin ran cold, and my body refused to stop shaking. My heart was racing so fast, I thought I was gonna pass out.

"Are you...you're talking about Dennis Snow? Is that what you're saying?" I asked.

"Are you alone? Are you alone?! If he hears me saying any of this he'll fucking kill me! He'll kill me! Please save me! Please get me out of here!" Walter sobbed.

"Walter, focus. I need you to answer my question."

"Yes! Dennis Snow kidnapped me. He's been torturing me. I did something bad. I did something really bad. That's why he kidnapped me."

I knew it. I had known it all along.

"What the hell did you do?"

"He even cut off my private parts. Oh god, it was so horrible. Why Dennis? Why? It was so painful. I screamed for hours, but no one can hear me here. That's what he kept telling me."

"Walter, what the hell did you do? Why did my Father kidnap you? Why is he torturing you? I need answers. I'm not helping you until I know what happened. I don't know what you've done to deserve all this," I urged.

For all I knew, he was an accomplice, or worse.

"I...I don't know. I don't know, I don't know, I don't know," Walter mumbled.

"Is my Father coming back soon?"

"Maybe, I don't know. He told me he had to take care of something and that he would be gone a while. I don't know. He doesn't tell me much. I miss Sandra, I miss my old life. I miss Violet."

Violet?

"There you go. He'll be gone a while. You need to explain to me why the fuck my Father has you locked up in a cellar. We're in an abandoned barn house in the middle of fucking nowhere. You said you did something really bad. Why do you miss my dead mother? Explain yourself, Walter," I said angrily.

"Okay," Walter sighed.

Walter began to explain the entire story through his eyes. Diamond's info had been accurate. My mother did cheat on my Father with Walter, numerous times. One night, Father was out of town, and I had taken Vera out to the mall. They finally made a careless mistake. My mother and Walter were kissing in front of an open window for just a few seconds. David had caught them. Walter later learned that David had been secretly watching them for my Father's sake. He left afterwards in his very recognizable 1998 Town Car.

"Shit, he saw us," Walter said.

"Don't worry, it'll be fine," Violet said.

"Are you sure? He's definitely going to tell Dennis, no question. You know how close they are. We're fucked."

"I need you to calm down and to go home to your wife before she grows suspicious."

"I think she already is. It doesn't take three hours to fix a closet."

"It does if it's a piece of crap."

They smiled at each other, uneasy. Two cheating spouses completely unaware of their grim futures and the violent chaos they would unleash onto themselves. That same night, Violet went to David's apartment. She brought him her famous homemade lemonade as a peace offering.

"I know what I saw, Violet. You're so lucky I couldn't call him. He's on the other side of the world. He'll kill me if I wake him up."

"David, let's consider things for a minute."

"I'm not considering anything. Walter already tried talking to me. I don't wanna hear it," David snapped.

"It's a lot better to say these things in person, David. You know that's the real reason you haven't called him."

"All I know is that you disgust me, and Dennis will finally realize what you are." David smirked.

"Can't we all discuss it together? I'll tell him myself, I promise. The day he comes back I will admit to cheating on him. You can be there if you wish," Violet offered.

"Really?"

"Yes really. If I don't keep my promise you can tell him anyway, you don't lose."

"Hmm, I don't know. I should tell him myself."

"I'm his wife, David. Please let me tell him. I need to be the one to tell him."

"Alright fine, but I want to be there. He'll need me there. He's going to be destroyed that you betrayed him like that," David said.

"I was destroyed when he betrayed me."

"How did he betray you?"

My mother remained silent for a few moments then answered.

"He betrayed me by promising to terrorize my life and my children's lives forever."

"You're a drama queen," David said as he chugged down the cup of lemonade my mother had made.

"This drama queen knows how to make good lemonade at least."

"You're a cheating piece of trash, but your *elixir* is still absolutely delicious, usually. This one tastes a little funny."

My mother left. She soon returned a few hours later with a spare key that Father had in his desk. My mother went inside, and saw David sprawled out on the floor, unmoving. She rushed over to him and felt his pulse. There wasn't one. He was dead. That had been my mother's plan all along. She had mixed in enough antifreeze into the lemonade to poison David and kill him. When she returned, she tied a rope around his neck. She planted him like he had committed suicide. Walter had helped her. She told him *everything*. My mother threatened Walter to help, or else she would tell Sandra about their affair along with another secret. A horribly dark secret that changed everything I thought I knew about myself.

They also planted an open bottle of antifreeze in the kitchen, and forged the suicide note with the phone number to cause misdirection.

"*I'm so sorry, but I had to do it. I hated you all.*"

My heart sunk all the way to the bottom of my stomach, I couldn't believe it. Uncle David never committed suicide. He was murdered, by my own mother. I had no idea my own mother was even capable of that. I couldn't believe she would go to such lengths to cover up her affair with Walter. A surge of rage boiled in my throat.

Why the hell didn't you kill Father? Oh mom, you could've saved us all.

"How the hell were you two never caught staging my uncle's suicide?"

"I don't know. We went very early in the morning, and tried to make as little noise as possible. Violet was fully prepared. She had the rope; the forged suicide note and various other things to not leave behind any DNA. We wore gloves, hairnets and plastic bags tied around our shoes. Violet was prepared. She wasn't about to get caught for murder. I just followed her lead, and kept my mouth shut. If I didn't help her, she told me she would've put his murder on me among other things. I was too afraid not to listen. There was a dead body in front of me," Walter coughed.

"Jesus," I muttered.

"Is he here? Is he here? If he's here we're dead. We're absolutely dead."

I closed my eyes, and focused my hearing. I heard nothing.

"He's not here. The stairs creak very loudly. I'll know when he's here."

"What will you do if he comes?"

"I'll split his head open with this sledgehammer."

"I hope you do it, it's the only way we'll survive."

"You still haven't explained how he kidnapped you, and how he found out."

"It all started years after David's death when he came back into to attend Caroline Duarte's funeral..."

Walter went to a bar after the funeral with some friends. Towards the end of the night, he ran into Father who happily greeted him. Walter had spoken with him at the funeral but didn't invite him out, he felt immense remorse over his affair with my mother. He was also an accomplice to David's staged suicide, so he was absolutely wracked with guilt. Regardless, Walter allowed Father to buy him several drinks. That turned out to be his ultimate downfall.

"Really sad funeral, huh? Caroline was a beautiful woman. So fucked up," Walter commented.

"Barry was a lucky man, I feel for him."

"When was the last time you were in town?"

"I don't even remember. After my brother died, life stopped for me. I don't keep track of much."

"I'm so sorry, Dennis, David was a good man."

"He was an even better brother. He was loyal and dependable. He was always on my side. I knew I could trust him for anything."

Walter downed a beer, and pointed at Dennis. He raised his eyebrows in curiosity.

"He drank her favorite lemonade before he passed. Did you know that?"

The beer that Walter was drinking had reminded him of the lemonade. He was nervous, and had no idea what to talk about.

"No, I didn't."

"Yeah it was Violet's. I've had it too. It's really good."

"I've tasted it, she knows her lemonade."

"She uh—, she had like a special name for this other type of lemonade she made. I forgot what it was."

My Father traced the outline of his cup with his finger, and ominously glared at Walter.

"*Violet's Vagina Elixir.*"

Walter snapped his finger.

"Yeees! That's the one!" Walter slurred.

"That's very interesting," Father whispered.

"What do you mean?"

"I know that he had antifreeze in his system because it was found at the crime scene. We assumed he wanted to ensure that he died. I always found that tidbit very odd. I didn't think he actually committed suicide in the first place, I always felt that someone had murdered him. It seems like the method of murder was poison."

"Oh."

"*Violet's Vagina Elixir*, huh?" Father mused.

"Yeah, that's it." Walter swallowed hard, and his heart was beating so fast he thought he was about to collapse.

"She only shared that special name with very special lovers, no one else." Father leaned over and gripped Walter's hands so hard, he felt the bones cracking. Walter wanted to scream, but Father put a finger to his lips.

"If you make a noise, I'll break your fucking hands," Father whispered.

Next thing he knew, he was outside in a dark alley. It was very late at night, and the streets were empty. Walter's friends were drunk, and had gone home. There wasn't a single soul in sight to witness Walter's ferocious beating. Father didn't hold back as he punched Walter's teeth in and forced the truth out of him. Walter confessed to everything. He admitted to sleeping with my mother, and to staging David's suicide. He told Father that my mother murdered David because she couldn't risk losing her part of Father's fortune.

She didn't want to have a messy divorce that would last years, and would potentially leave her with nothing. She wanted *something* after dealing with Father's abuse for so many years. She felt she was owed that. A part of me also felt that my mother killed David because she secretly hated him, and had wanted my Father to suffer. I always knew that my family was very complicated. That turned out to be an understatement.

"He kidnapped you as revenge."

"He did, and he's been torturing me ever since. He says he has big plans for the rest of his family. He says you're the most stubborn of them all."

"Fuck. What big plans?"

I'm not surprised. I knew something was coming.

"I don't know. I don't think he expected you to find this place yet."

"Did that twisted bastard confess to butchering my family?"

"He killed Violet. He killed Violet because she murdered David. He told me it had been a rage-filled murder that he had thoroughly enjoyed. He enjoyed it so much he wanted to do it again."

"My god, he's a fucking monster."

"I'm so sorry Venus. I was fooled by who he was in the outside world. I had no idea he had this horrible darkness inside of him. I never suspected him to be like this, ever."

I collapsed to the ground and stared at the floor. My tears dripped to the ground, and I let them. I had been right all along. I should've felt relief, but relief from what? That I had been right about my

Father being a deranged killer? It was so twisted I couldn't put it into words. No one in the world had the life I had, I was alone.

My Father was a killer who had murdered my mother. He chopped her head off with an axe and displayed her severed head as a trophy in an open field. My life was truly something to behold. At least I knew why my Father had murdered my mother. I now knew I could trust Walter. He wasn't Father's accomplice; he was his prisoner.

"He is a very sick person, Venus. He is a sadistic psychopath who forces me to listen to his stories on how he murdered your family. It has turned my heart into ice. I have cried, and suffered so much. I gave up on my life. I accepted my fate, until you came. You made me cry. I haven't cried in a long time."

"How do I free you?"

"Don't free me," Walter whispered.

"Why?"

"You haven't asked me about Vanya and Vera," Walter choked.

"Father killed them," I snapped.

Walter remained quiet.

"Right?" I asked.

"The horrible secret, the one that's been kept from you, is that I am your father," Walter confessed.

My heart began palpitating, and my breathing grew shallow.

"What the hell are you talking about?" I asked angrily.

"Your mother and I had our affair for years, Venus. I'm so sorry. She threatened to tell Dennis that fact, if I didn't help kill David with her.

She hated David that much, and wanted to cause that much suffering to Dennis, for everything she had gone through," Walter explained.

After everything, Walter had been my true father. It wasn't that crazy to consider, they had their affair for years on end. As insane as it sounded, I believed it.

"Well, that's just great isn't it? More reason to believe that I was born cursed, into a family filled with pain, death, murder and severed heads," I hissed.

But that ends now.

"Venus, I have something else to tell you," Walter said softly.

"How many damn secrets do you have, old man?!"

"When I tell you, I won't be surprised if you decide to split me in half with whatever weapon you happen to find," Walter admitted.

"*What?*"

"I...I...I murdered Vera and Vanya," Walter confessed.

"What?" I squeaked out.

"I'm so sorry," Walter sobbed.

"You...you're nothing!" I shrilled.

I landed the sledgehammer on Walter's left foot, crushing several of his fungal-infected toenails, causing it to bleed. He wailed in pain.

"I deserve it, I deserve it, I deserve it," Walter mumbled.

"You're coming with me, you're going to answer for this," I demanded.

"But, wait, I need to tell you—" Walter trailed, as I shut his mouth by back handing his dry, cracked lips.

"No more talking," I commanded.

I winded back the sledgehammer and swung it towards the metal clasps that held the chain in place., I fiercely hit it several times until it broke off. Walter fell forward, and I dragged him up.

"Please just kill me now, I know you want to do it. I understand, I've sinned, I've sinned horribly. All those years have caught up to me, all of these karmic consequences," Walter cried.

"You're not getting off that easy, you sick fuck."

"Wait! What if he's here? What if he's arrived? We're dead if he's here!"

"Move your ass!"

I aggressively dragged Walter up the stairs as he grunted with every step. By the time we reached the top of the stairs, he was winded. He doubled over, and was desperately gasping for air. After a few minutes, I helped him slide forward. We were in the barn house, and the coast was clear.

"He's not here, *dad*. But, you don't need to worry about him, you need to worry about *me*," I threatened.

"I'm sorry I never told you, I'm sorry it had to be this way. But, I was forced to kill them, I swear," Walter pleaded.

"What are you talking about?"

"I killed Caroline too, I helped Barry. I'm nothing, I'm absolutely nothing."

"What do you mean you killed Caroline?!"

"I'm a serial killer, aren't I? I'm so sorry. I'm sorry that your own father is a serial killer," Walter whispered.

A sharp, distinctive *pop* sliced through the air, and whizzed past my head. When I turned, a chunk of Walter's head was missing. It had exploded onto the ground. He was rapidly moving his mouth, and tongue for a few terror-stricken moments before abruptly falling down. I screamed so loud it echoed off the walls. I sprinted towards cover, and hid behind the Firebird as three more gunshots rang out. I immediately slid out my phone in a matter of seconds. Arthur had responded. I had a very brief moment of relief.

"Jesus Christ, Venus. I'm really mad at you right now. You should've told me. I'm on my way. Stay safe and don't die. I'm serious, Venus. Don't you fucking die on me. We have a kid to raise. I'm not doing it without you."

I won't die, Arthur. I promise you.

"So you finally figured it out. You crazy, stubborn bitch," Father boomed.

"You motherfucker," I whispered to myself as I wiped the bullets of sweat rolling down my forehead.

"There's no one here to save you, baby girl. You're next."

I knew. I knew it all along. I was next.

CHAPTER 19
25 YEARS EARLIER

I was alone in my room when I felt a heavy presence in front of me. I had been sleeping. It was dark. I heard ominous breathing, and my eyes flew open. I froze in complete terror when I saw who was in front of me. It was Father. I whimpered and pulled up the covers to hide my face. He aggressively tore it back down and leaned in. I was terrified of moving. I barely breathed to remain still.

"You need to stay quiet, little girl. Do you understand me?" Father commanded.

"Okay."

"You need to stop calling me a monster. No one will *ever* believe you. I'll have them think you're insane. I could murder you in cold blood and no one would ever suspect it was me. I'm a respected man in St. Devil. You are *nothing*."

I didn't say anything and just nodded. I had no idea what I had done to deserve that treatment from Father. I didn't think drawing monsters around my room would drive him to act like a psychopath. I should've known better, but I had to show the world what Father truly was in my own way. Unfortunately, no one ever believed me.

"We're going to the *Box*," Father growled.

It was like he had a split personality. I thought of him as Dr. Jekyll and Mr. Hyde as I grew older. I had my eyes shut the entire ride over to the *Box* except when we got off. I saw the abandoned barn house. I saw Optic Drive. That's what I was trying to remember. That was the memory that refused to resurface, among others. I had never truly forgotten any of that...I just buried it so deep in my mind it was like it never existed. That's what trauma did to me. It made me conceal my pain until I refused to accept what had happened. If I did accept it...it would've destroyed me.

Next thing I knew I was tied to a wooden beam in a dark, concrete prison. He used a leather belt to hit me. He hit me hard enough to make me scream out in anguish, but not hard enough to leave any lasting marks. My wounds always healed on the outside, but they remained inside me to act as a cruel reminder of what I had gone through.

"Why do you call me a monster?"

"I don't know. I'm sorry dad," I trembled.

I can't tell you because you'll kill me. You'll finally do it dad. You will kill me.

"Why do you call me a monster?!" Father whacked me across the face, and I began sobbing.

"Please dad, please stop."

"I'm good friends with the director of the Harrington Psychiatric Institute. I donate a lot of money and my own father, Declan Snow, was hospitalized for ten long years. Declan apparently means 'full of goodness.' My father was the complete opposite. He made life hell for me and my brother. We only had each other. I'll spin a tale to the director that you've been harming yourself. I'll tell him that I'm very concerned because our family has a history of severe mental illness."

I knew from an early age that Father was my mental illness. He never let me *be* and didn't allow me to express myself the way I wanted to. He was a tyrant.

"Please stop this. I want to go home."

"You're very stubborn. I hate that about you," Father clucked his tongue.

"Why do you hate me so much dad? Why?"

"No! You can't win against me, Venus. You can't!"

"Win what?! I'm your daughter! You shouldn't be hitting me. You should love me. I'm your freaking daughter!" I shouted.

"Scream like that again and I'll yank out your teeth, one by one, and then I'll carve out your tongue. You'll never talk again," Father threatened.

One day you'll be gone, and my life will be normal. One day. I can't wait.

I was so young and already wishing death on my Father. I blamed him for most of my mental issues and my frenzied anxiety attacks. It was all because of him. He suppressed my very being. He never allowed me to have a normal childhood. He robbed me of that. All he did was belittle me, control me, and abuse me. I was his punching bag. I promised myself that one day I wouldn't be, and the day did come.

CHAPTER 20
PRESENT DAY

It was the end. It had finally arrived. Father shot at the car, and I cringed with every shot. I was having my worst anxiety attack yet. It was crippling me, but I had to move. I had to. If I didn't, I was dead meat. I put one leg in front of the other, and used the car as leverage to slide myself away from Walter's dead body. I reached the front end of the car, and crawled behind a stack of wooden barrels. I had trouble breathing, and my heart was pummeling my chest into oblivion. I had never been more scared in my entire life. Death was looming across from me, and one false move meant I was gone forever.

I placed down the sledgehammer on the floor, and took out my knife to wield it. The sledgehammer was too heavy, and was slowing me down. I needed to be quick. The shots were getting closer. I sensed it. The bullets were ricocheting louder, and louder off the car's exterior. I thought about what to do.

If I made a run for it, he would surely kill me, or shoot a vital body part. If I stayed put he was going to reach me, and put a bullet in my brain. I used the information I had from reporting true crime. I thought about how most serial killers liked to talk about their murders. They loved the attention, they craved it. They secretly wanted to confess everything they had done. That's why Kenneth Kilhouser had almost confessed to me. More than anything, I didn't go that far just to die, I needed to know the whole truth. I needed to know how he was connected to everything.

"Why? Why did you kill my mother?! My aunt?! My sister?! Tell me, dad. Why?!" I ferociously shouted.

"Violet, your mother, started it all. She murdered my little brother, David. She *murdered* him because she didn't want me to know the truth. My own brother! My own blood! I was supposed to protect him!"

"You were supposed to protect us!"

Father stopped shooting, I heard the soft crunch of hay beneath his feet as he slowly crept towards me.

"I have always wanted to kill, I wanted to know how it felt. When I found out David was murdered by Violet, I didn't hesitate for a single moment. I wanted revenge. So, I kidnapped Walter, and took his car. We went for a long ride to the middle of nowhere. His own friends were too busy partying, and drinking to notice. No one was the wiser. I scooped out his eyeballs, and chopped off his manhood for using it to fuck my whore of a wife for so long."

"You're fucking sick," I crawled further away from the sound of his crunching footsteps. I desperately attempted to remain in cover.

"I can't believe you found this place. I'll admit it, I tried to give you a clue once I knew you were getting close. The location from the "anonymous" source...the eyeballs...Walter's belongings...his manhood. All a bit on the nose, but I thought you'd appreciate the assistance."

He had known all along. He wanted me to find him.

"Why did you let me live? Why did you let me live after all these years? Why did you murder all of them except me?"

"I knew that you were the only one stubborn enough, smart enough, and motivated enough to expose me as St. Devil's serial killer. You didn't disappoint, baby girl."

"Don't fucking call me that. You're nothing to me!"

"I don't feel the same way, you're everything to me," Father appeared behind the car, and pointed his rifle. I saw him from a minuscule crack between two wooden barrels. I quickly crawled further away towards a haystack.

"How the fuck am I everything to you? You beat me, you abused me, you made me feel like I was nothing, you almost destroyed me."

"Don't blame me, blame your mother."

"You were a violent bastard before David's death. You only got worse afterwards. Don't fucking act like you were some saint."

"I only act like a saint because people are quick to believe that I am one, I know how to play the part and I play it well."

"A lot of people make a big fucking mistake."

"Christ, you sound just like your mother."

"Better her than you. She tried to stop you, and for her, I'll do what she couldn't."

"No one ever suspects the good rich husband, Venus. There is no stopping me. If that were the case, I would've been dead a long time ago."

"I always suspected it was you, and I was right."

"What good did that do? You're about to be a dead woman."

"You're not going to kill me, not today," I whispered.

"Once I chopped off your whore mother's head, I wanted to do it again. Putting you women in your place was the best thrill I ever had. Fuck business, or sex. When I realized that I had a reason to kill, I didn't wait. I did what I had always wanted to do."

"You're a depraved bastard."

"I am a depraved bastard, just like Barry Duarte. Good job by the way. I knew he murdered his wife. It was obvious that he had grown sick of her," Father said calmly.

"Just because you get sick of someone doesn't mean you kill them. What the fuck is wrong with you people? You're both less than human for what you've done!"

"What about Walter? He helped Barry kill his own wife Caroline, and for what? For drugs!" Father shouted.

That was why he had done it. Walter had helped Barry murder Caroline, for drugs. That was why they had been good friends. They had cruelty in common.

"You're all the worst this world has to offer," I said softly.

"Let's not forget about Violet either. Is she not less than human for what she did to my brother?! She poisoned him to hide what she did to me! She's nothing!"

"Why did Walter kill Aunt Vanya and my sister, Vera?! What the fuck did they ever do to him?!" I yelled.

"You ask a lot of questions for someone who's about to die."

"There couldn't be a better time."

"I wanted revenge against Walter because he had helped murder David, and because of his betrayal. I wanted him to suffer, endlessly."

"What did you do?"

"It was easy, Vanya always liked me. That was obvious."

"Only because she didn't know the real you," I hissed.

You sick son of a bitch.

"I'm good at hiding things," Father laughed.

"I can't believe you're laughing at this. You're a psychopath!" I slithered on the ground towards some more piles of hay, but hiding spots were running out. It was only a matter of time before I had to do something.

"It was vengeance, Venus. I only did what needed to be done, I had Vanya invite me over. I knew what she wanted, she wanted me. I brought over what I needed, to make it quick. Vera was gone so that helped. I drugged Vanya, by putting something in her drink. I learned from the best, Violet. Once she was knocked out, I touched her as much as I wanted. You don't understand the thrill that gave me. I had Walter with me as well, I made him do as I commanded."

I had to swallow my stomach bile, as it almost shot out of my throat. I couldn't believe what I was hearing.

"She was right. You are a fucking narcissist."

"I won't apologize for liking to talk about my work. The only ones who can listen are the ones who are about to die."

"You're the one who's going to fucking die!" I threatened.

"You should've been there when Vanya woke up. I was dressed up in all black with my axe in hand. Before she screamed, Walter slit her throat. I wanted him to kill an innocent, and I wanted him to suffer. I needed him to kill the woman who was his secret lover's sister. That was justice. I then cleanly sliced her head off. It plopped to the floor like a bowling ball, and I collected my trophy. You see, Barry was too unstable. He was never going to get away with Caroline's murder. He wasn't careful like me. Walter knew that as well. It's a shame Barry didn't give him up, but the dead don't speak do they?"

"You're the fucking devil, your mind has rotted with nothing but evil. Why Vera? What did Vera ever do to you?!"

"Vera was a case of wrong place, wrong time. She saw everything when she came in. I thought she was sleeping over a friend's house, but her plans changed. So my plan had to change as well."

"No..." I trailed.

"She cried and begged for mercy as I chased after her. I couldn't have any witnesses. She begged so much for her life, and told me that despite everything, she loved me. Those were the last words she said before I held her down, and had Walter cut her throat open. He helped me as I slashed her head away from her body. He's just as guilty in the murders of your family, as I am."

"*No!*" A furious, guttural screech shot out of my mouth as pure adrenaline surged through my veins. I sprinted towards Father with my fingers tightly wrapped around my knife.

He smiled, pointed his rifle, and shot. Every single moment in my entire life had led to that moment. To the moment where I would inevitably face off with my Father and destroy him for everything he had done to me.

I was going to erase him for all the abuse, torment, violence and pain he had caused me over so many years. He was the reason I was in and out of a mental institution for ten years. He was the reason why my mother had become a bitter, unloving woman. He was the reason why my beautiful, funny Aunt Vanya and my sweet, innocent sister Vera were dead. He was the reason why I had been capable of fostering so much hate in my heart that it turned to ice. It was dedicated to him, and only him.

He was the reason for all my grief, and all my suffering. I was finally going to do something about it. Whether he died or we both died, it would end that day on that hour in that horrible place that I had known so many years ago. He didn't get to win. *Monsters never win.*

Bang.

I collapsed to the ground underneath him. Blood was dripping from my ear. He shot off a good chunk of it, and all I heard was a metallic ringing that dulled my senses for a few seconds. I looked up, and saw him staring down at me with a devilish grin. He was saying something, but it came out muffled and low. When I regained use of my body, without thinking, I swung my arm towards Father's leg, and plunged my knife as deep as I could into his thigh. He let out a pained yell, and fell forward. The rifle flew out of his hands, and landed a few feet away from us.

"You...you fucking bitch. You're dead. You hear me? *You are fucking dead!*" Father foamed at the mouth with so much ferocity, and anguish that the mask finally flew off. The monster had been unveiled, and it was terrifying.

I quickly crawled away, and lunged towards the rifle. Father's hand shot out, and grabbed my foot. My heart imploded in my chest as I screamed, and fell forward. I kicked, and kicked until his beastly hand was off of me. I continued to hastily crawl forward until I reached the rifle. I fumbled it as I picked it up but managed to get a grip. I stepped backwards until I hit a stack of barrels, I pointed the rifle at my Father's face. He laughed like a maniac, he laughed like how I knew he would.

"Violet, Vanya, Vera, Barry, Caroline, Walter, and David are all dead. The whole family line is done for. It's only you, and me who are left. Let's fucking end it all, Venus. There's no point to any of this anymore. Let's finish what I started, let's end this cycle of pain, and violence forever."

"You're a fucking psycho. You're responsible for killing all of them, you motherfucker. You took my family away from me!" I growled.

"Your mother took David away from me! My only brother! She cheated on me with Walter, and then murdered him because he saw! Because he witnessed! David's only crime was being a loyal brother. You tell me how that's fucking fair, Venus! *Tell me!*" Father yelled with tears in his eyes.

"Don't you dare, don't fucking cry. You sick piece of shit. You were supposed to love me, and take care of me. You were the worst dad ever, you killed Vera, your own daughter. Can you explain to me why you did that?! *Fucking explain that to me!*"

"After David died, I wanted you all dead. It gave me a reason to slaughter. The thrill was unlike anything I had ever experienced before. I have demons inside me, Venus, and you do too."

"You're insane, you should've been the one in that asylum."

"Go on with it. I want you to end it, Venus, I want you to kill me."

"I will."

My finger slowly went to the trigger.

"I'm done anyway, I finished what I set out to do."

"Yeah, no shit."

"I went to your home, I wanted to pay you a visit. Only Arthur was there. He was spooked to see me, he looked like he was in a hurry. He told me you needed help. That's why I came here, Venus. Your husband put up a good fight. I think he said he loved you. I couldn't exactly understand what he was saying because he was choking on his own blood. It's a shame. I liked Arthur. I left you a piece of him outside."

I let out a bestial, animalistic scream that ravaged my throat.

"He should've never invited me inside. The fear he had of offending me was greater than the fear he had for his own life."

"No, no, no, no, no, no, no, no, no. You're lying, you're fucking lying. Tell me you're fucking lying!" I screamed.

"End your life, Venus. You'll end all the suffering, and all the pain," Father took out the knife that was lodged in his leg, and yelled.

"What are you—,"

"Goodbye, Venus. Do what you need to do. Finish what I started, end your life. There's nothing left for you, destroy the family line forever."

Father closed his eyes, and plunged the knife into his neck. My knees buckled, and I almost fell out of sheer shock. Father held the knife there as all his blood rushed out like a red waterfall. He held it there until he fell back, and died. I tossed away the rifle, and slowly approached him. He was finally dead. After so many years, Father was dead. In the end I didn't kill him, and I was relieved about that. I didn't need any more demons in me, and I didn't need anymore darkness clouding my head.

I ran outside as a searing pain flared up in what was left of my right ear. The sun was setting as an orange streak of light was slowly fading across the horizon. I gazed at it in relief. It was all over. The adrenaline was wearing off, and I needed help. I quickly called nine-one-one, and was able to get a signal for a few seconds before the call dropped. I hoped they would come. A volley of panic churned in my stomach when I spotted it. There was a black trash bag in the middle of the field. It was a few yards away from where I stood.

No...no it can't be. Oh my god, Arthur.

I sprinted towards the bag, and reached it in seconds. I quickly undid the knot, and checked inside. The smell of hot blood, and flesh was powerfully repulsive. I couldn't tell what was inside so lifted the bag up, and let the contents spill out. I dropped to my knees in complete horror.

A volcanic burning sensation whirled inside me as I puked my guts out. I sobbed, and wailed at the top of my lungs as I stared at Arthur's detached head. Father had told the truth. He had murdered him too. My poor Arthur. The man that I had loved for so long. Father had robbed me yet again. He took away the possibility of a happy life with the man I had dearly loved. He robbed me of having a joyous, little family with Arthur.

He would never rob me ever again, he was forever gone. I cried my heart out until I heard the sirens of the police, and ambulances racing towards me. It was the worst pain I had experienced since the murders of my family. I thought about it. I thought about ending it all. All I had to do was run inside, get the rifle, and shoot myself in the head. I did that, and the nightmare that was my life would finally be over.

No, I wouldn't let him win. I had to live. I had to live for my mother, for Aunt Vanya, for Vera, for Arthur, and for my baby. I had to go on. I had kept my promise.

Monsters never win.

CHAPTER 21

The next few days after my final, deadly confrontation with Dennis Snow were a foggy haze. I couldn't call him Father anymore because he wasn't my dad. Walter was my father, but none of that mattered anymore. My true father was a serial killer, and so was Dennis Snow.

I was in the hospital being evaluated. My room was comfortable and straightforward. I had an adjustable mattress, and the TV was playing elevator music. It felt like I was in the waiting room for heaven. I almost wished I was. Being in the hospital left me feeling depressed because of its dull white colors, and bright lights. I also had nothing to do but think about everything that had happened a million times over.

Thankfully they stitched up my ear, and it didn't look too bad. There was a chunk of it missing but at the very least I was *alive*. My baby was alive too, miraculously. When I was first taken to the hospital they ran many tests. That's when they realized I was pregnant. They checked if the baby had a heartbeat, and it did, I was lucky. After going through that very strenuous, and violent confrontation with my Father I thought I had lost the baby.

It had been my stubborn choice regardless. I was not raising my baby with the serial killer still standing. It just so happened that I had been proven right. The serial killer behind the *St. Devil Beheadings* had been Dennis. I should've felt relieved after everything that had happened, but I was hurting, badly. Arthur was dead, he was my rock. He was my heart and soul. I didn't know what I was gonna do without him. The idea that I would have to one day tell my baby that her father had been murdered by her grandfather was beyond twisted. She'd eventually find out about her deeply disturbing family history as well. It was something that should've never happened, but it did, and I had to live with that.

I would also have to explain the murders of my mother, aunt, and sister. It wasn't a conversation I was looking forward to. I considered ending it all for a brief moment, but no. I was going to live on for them. I was going to live on for my family. I wouldn't allow Dennis' deranged ambitions to come to fruition. I wouldn't destroy the family line. I would save it, and I would continue it. I would root out the curse that had caused so much pain and death.

I wanted to be the person who purged the tragedies, and traumas from the Snow family's history. I wanted future generations to live in peace, and happiness because after so much hate, pain, violence, death, and suffering, they deserved it. I deserved it.

There was a knock at the door. It was Detective Peter Jurgen. He slowly entered. He had been involved in David's case.

"Hey Venus."

"Hi."

"I just wanted to see how you were doing." Detective Jurgen came closer and sat on a chair next to me.

"I'm doing okay, considering the circumstances."

"I can't even begin to imagine, Venus. I am so, so sorry. It's—, it's unbelievable. It's insane. Dennis Snow turns out to be the serial killer behind the *St. Devil Beheadings*. A respected, and charitable businessman in St. Devil's community slaughtered his own family. My god."

"Yeah, my supposed father."

"Listen Venus, I came by because I wanted to let you know that the press will be after you like hound dogs. I got some old buddies of mine to escort you home when it's time for you to go. They're not retired."

"I appreciate that a lot, Detective Jurgen. Thank you."

"It's the least I can do, I've been following the case a bit. I'm happy you turned out okay."

"Me too."

I'm glad that at least someone came to talk to me about the whole thing. In truth, I had absolutely no one when Arthur died. He was the only person I really talked to, and loved after my family's tragic deaths.

"A buddy of mine told me that they're gonna give you some time before they start asking questions. This is a very extreme situation. There was a lot of deaths, murders, they're gonna take it easy," Detective Jurgen explained.

"Thank you, I need that."

All I want is easy right now.

"You're also gonna have to wait at least two weeks before going back home," Detective Jurgen said softly.

"Why?"

"Arthur was tragically killed inside your home, I'm so sorry, Venus."

"I understand," I nodded.

"Do you want to talk about it?"

"I don't," I choked back a sob.

I couldn't think about him too much, I'd start wailing.

Detective Jurgen had been right. There were dozens of reporters grouped up outside my house. A flurry of news vans were lined up and down the whole street. It was madness. Detective Jurgen and 4 other police officers drove home. They shielded me as the reporters surrounded us and hurled a barrage of questions towards me.

What happened to Dennis Snow? Why were there reports of gunshots in Devil's Orchard?

Is it true that Walter Campbell was kidnapped and murdered? Can you confirm that?

Is it true that you were hunting down your father because you suspected him of being the serial killer?

There are rumors that your father built a disturbing torture dungeon. Does this dungeon actually exist?

So many individuals in your family have been murdered. This includes your former brother-in-law Barry Duarte. Now it seems that your husband Arthur Duarte was also killed recently inside your own home. Are all of these deaths connected?

I was able to get inside and quickly locked the door. Detective Jurgen and the other officers slowly but surely got everyone to leave. I immediately went to my bedroom and laid down in my bed. I picked up a blanket that had been on his side and smelled it. It smelled like him. I used it to wipe the waterworks that were spilling out of my eyes. A world without Arthur was a scary one, and not one I was ready to live in.

Dennis Snow, David Snow, Violet Snow, Vanya Reyes, Vera Snow, Barry Duarte, Caroline Duarte, Arthur Duarte, all dead and gone. Despite the unimaginable tragedy that I had gone through, I needed to stay strong for my future baby. First I needed to allow myself to grieve Arthur's death. I needed to get past that pain, and suffering before I'd be able to function as a person again. I remained bedridden for weeks while my phone continued to blow up every day. I had offers for interviews, collaborations, documentary features, and many other things I didn't feel like doing.

After two days, I was able to muster up the strength to eat more than one meal a day. I had to for the baby. After five days, Arthur's funeral arrangements needed to be put in order. I paid for it all, but I refused to attend. I was sick, and tired of funerals. I wanted to mourn him alone, and in my own way. I went out to my backyard, and sat on my tire swing. I had a notebook with me, and a balloon. I wrote Arthur a letter.

"Arthur...I never imagined losing you. I don't know how I'm going to carry on without you. You were my rock throughout our entire relationship together. You were always there. I took that for granted. I sincerely regret not being able to raise our child together. I know you wanted a family with me more than anything else in the world and in the end I wanted it too. I swear to you. I wanted to be a mom and I wanted you to be a dad. Please know that I will raise our child in a house full of love, peace, and happiness like we would've done together. I'm breaking the cycle of terror and abuse. My child will not grow up with any monsters haunting their nightmares. I love you, Arthur. I'll see you again someday."

I tied the note around the balloon, and released it to the sky. It floated up, and up until I lost sight of it. I remained on the tire swing, and reminisced about the good times I had with Arthur. I thought about the happy times we could've experienced together, and grieved because it would never happen.

I was flipping through old pictures of Arthur, and I in the living room. They were pictures from our marriage. We were so happy in those photos, I cherished having them. There was a knock at the door that broke me out of my cheerful trance. I rushed towards it, and hoped it wasn't another reporter. I had turned away about thirty over the span of just one week. When I looked through the peephole it was the detective. The one that Jurgen told me would visit. I prepared myself to explain everything that had happened. I opened the door, and invited the detective in. Once we exchanged pleasantries, I started from the beginning. By the end of it all, his face was deeply etched with worry, and concern. I assured him that everything would be alright. Detective Jurgen had said it himself, I was too stubborn to die.

I found myself at my desk in deep thought. I was planning on writing a piece about my family's history. I wanted to write about their lives, and what it meant for me when I found out Dennis, and Walter were the killers that destroyed them all. One had been my father figure, and the other was my actual father. I wasn't sure if I was gonna publish it, but I wanted to get it done.

I needed to see it as a tragic series of events from the past so I could move on. When I finished it, that would be it. That time in my life would be erased from memory, I would choose to no longer reflect on it. I didn't want to, I only wanted to reflect on the good memories. Those were the only memories worth remembering.

Something the police found in one of Dennis' properties was a letter to someone I never expected. It was the letter that had been in his wooden chest at his lakehouse. The one I didn't see, the one he didn't want me to see. He had lied to me, it wasn't a letter to David. It was a letter to Kenneth Kilhouser. It had been there the whole time. It stated his thanks for inspiring him to take the heads off his female victims to use as trophies. Dennis liked the idea of leaving his mark. He seemed to idolize Kilhouser. I planned to write the parallels that Dennis Snow and Kenneth Kilhouser had. I also found out that Kenneth used to do maintenance for properties that Dennis owned. I wondered if they ever discussed their twisted murder fantasies with each other. I wondered if Kenneth Kilhouser had been the man who implanted the twisted idea in Dennis' head, the idea of slaughtering our entire family.

Dennis was the monster who had haunted my nightmares for a long time. It took absolutely everything I had, but I destroyed him once and for all. I finally eradicated the man who made my entire life a living hell since the day I was born, but at a great cost.

The cost of all my loved ones. Despite that, I would go on. I would show everyone that there was still light even in the darkest of times. I would act as a living reminder that monsters never won.

EPILOGUE

"I loved the idea that you saw me, fully intent on killing you and there was not a single thing you could do about it. You were helpless. You couldn't run, scream, or hide. It was too late. I was inches away from your terrified face and before you could even blink, you were finished forever. I only wish that I had done it much, much earlier and that you were somehow able to see how I butchered the people you loved most."

One of many private tapes that Dennis Snow recorded while he lurked inside the *Box*, his own personal murder dungeon. They were found by the police, and that one in particular had been leaked online. Venus wished she had the power to remove it. She made sure none of the other tapes ever saw the light of day. The other tapes explicitly stated how Dennis tortured Walter, and how he made him comply with his gruesome beheadings. No one needed to listen to that, and no one else needed inspiration.

It was a brisk, windy morning when Venus went to the St. Devil cemetery. She navigated through greenery, and a narrow pathway that included rows of gravestones. She eventually reached Dennis Snow's tombstone. It was hidden between two towering trees. Venus had done that on purpose. It had piles of leaves draped all over it, and Venus wouldn't want anything different. She spat on it.

"Your terror is over. I need you to know that. You never would've won. I kept my promise to Vera. I stopped you for her, and for everyone else you killed. I'm going to live a happy life just to spite you. Goodbye forever."

Venus turned her head, and saw Arthur in the distance, smiling at her. She turned back, and closed her eyes. Venus' heart was thumping hard against her chest. She knew it wasn't true. She had changed for the better. She no longer saw things that weren't there. She focused on living in the present. Once she said her final goodbye to the man who nearly killed her, she completed what she had set out to do. She was onto to the next phase of her life which was preparing to raise her newborn daughter, Victoria "Vera" Duarte.

When she looked back at where Arthur was, he was gone. She smiled to herself and walked away forever. She never returned to that burial ground, and never planned to, for all time.

THE END.

THANK YOU!

Thanks so much for reading *MY FATHER IS A SERIAL KILLER*! If you liked this book, be sure to stay subscribed to my newsletter for free books, updates about future books and more! Visit spencergu erreroauthor.com to sign up! Please consider leaving a review! I read them all! It helps me immensely as an author!

MY SON IS A MURDERER, MY WIFE'S STALKER and *A MURDER IN THE NEIGHBORHOOD* are also available in paperback/digital formats on Amazon and on Kindle Unlimited!

SHOUT-OUTS

I want to give a huge shout out and thanks to my family for supporting me and encouraging me throughout my long journey of wanting to be a writer and an author. Mom, Dad, Sebastian, and Sophia. There has been a lot of ups and downs. There were even times where I wanted to give up and was frustrated beyond understanding. You could've easily shot down my dreams and tell me that I would never make it. That has never been the case and I'm very lucky for that. I love you guys and I appreciate you!

There are a lot of other people who have in one way or another, have given me words of encouragement and support in other ways. Please know that I appreciate you all! You keep me going. To my readers, you are the lifeline. You are the reason I write books. You are the reason why I'm so passionate to get these stories out there. I'm very lucky to have you all. I read and appreciate every single review beyond measure. I love books so much and I love being able to share mine with you all!

A BIG thank you to all Facebook Book Groups for your support!
Psychological Thriller Readers, Psychological Thrillers Book Club,
Sarah's Book Club, Domestic Thrillers Book Club, Tattered Page Book
Club.

ABOUT THE AUTHOR

My name is Spencer Guerrero and I am a screenwriter and novelist. I've written over a dozen short stories and over twenty screenplays. This includes short films, feature film scripts, animated scripts and book adaptations. I was hired to complete some of these works for numerous clients and small production companies. My feature-length, teen comedy screenplay titled *HEATHER CHANG DECLARES WAR* placed top 100 in a screenplay contest. My favorite genres are YA, mystery-thriller, fantasy and literary fiction. Other than that, I like funny cat memes and I play basketball.